# THE FOG ROLLS IN

by Naida Webster

This is a work of fiction. Names, characters, places and incidences are either a product of the author's imagination or are used fictitiously. Any resemblance to actual persons, living or dead, events, or locales is entirely coincidental.

Copyright© 2016 Naida Webster
All rights reserved
ISBN-13: 978-1539031673
ISBN-10: 1539031675

ALSO BY NAIDA JOY WEBSTER
*on Amazon*

The Phantom of Kenton High (2014)
Summer of Torment (2014)
Missing Anna (2015)
Stranger at my Door (2016)

# Chapter 1

Janene Dawson set the heavy suitcase down with a thud, glancing at her watch, noting it was 1:00 am, then quickly consulted the information chart that hung above the terminal entrance. "Damn," she muttered wearily as she read the imposing fact that the last limousine had left the terminal nearly twenty minutes earlier and that there would not be another until six o'clock.

She stood hesitantly, her brow furrowed as she considered her plight. She had disembarked at the Los Angeles International Airport from the Trailways bus just a few minutes before. She was tired and wanted nothing more at that moment than to be comfortably snuggled into her bed in her plush Santa Ana apartment. Instead, here she was stranded in a virtually empty airport terminal for five hours. Her slim lithe figure slumped tiredly as she stood there alone balancing precariously on one foot as she wriggled her other foot free from the heeled pump she wore. Her feet hurt and she was bone tired. Her short blonde hair waved attractively about her oval face. Wearily, she brushed an escaping curl back from her face.

There were no seats available despite the fact that she was practically alone. She looked forlornly at the closed information booth allowing her glance to wander beyond and down the lengthy grey-walled corridor which led to the coffee shop and the flight passenger waiting room.

She turned slightly to gaze outside the terminal entrance into the darkness broken only by a dim street lamp beyond. 'What a night, what a trip!' she thought glumly. She had flown in from Portland, Oregon on a routine three hour flight which had so far taken her 16 hours. Not only had her bus trip from her home in the small mid-eastern Washington town taken her four hours but she'd had a three hour layover before connecting with her flight to Los Angeles. Then L. A. International Airport had been fogged in and her plane had landed instead in Ontario. The airlines had bussed the passengers from Ontario to Los Angeles which had taken another hour and half. After finally arriving, she was to learn the airport limousine service suspended operation at 12:30 a. m..

She had two choices since it would cost a fortune to hire a taxi to take her from the airport to her apartment in Santa Ana. She could either sit here on her suitcase until six in the morning or take the long hike down the corridor and wait in the coffee shop. Neither idea particularly appealed to her. Since no flights were arriving nor departing from the airport until the fog cloud lifted, the terminal was virtually closed. All the passenger waiting rooms were shut off and dark which left only the coffee shop or the baggage terminal open. She was too unfamiliar with the terminal and too weary to venture far and there seemed to be no comfortable place to retire for her long wait.

Glumly, she deposited her purse on the floor beside her suitcase and sat down on the latter balancing carefully. She rested an elbow on her knees supporting her chin on the palm of her hand. How long she had sat thusly she was uncertain. Her mind was blank, her eyes staring unseeingly into space.

She was startled into alertness by a low, husky male voice asking, "Are you all right, miss?" She looked up in confusion at the tall, dark rugged man who stood bending toward her, his face mirroring genuine concern.

"Oh, yes," she stammered. "I'm fine, really I am. Thank you." A weary half smile flitted across her face as she rose to her feet.

"You look as if you've lost your last friend," her companion added drily.

" I haven't really, " she explained. "More accurately I'm tired and thoroughly disgusted." She continued waspishly not wanting to explain further and silently wishing he'd just go away.

"I noticed you were on that Ontario flight. I'm rather disgusted myself. This fog cloud is a damn inconvenience to say the least. Where are you headed?"

"Santa Ana," she answered briefly. She observed his quick glance toward the information chart but turned away from him.

"So you're stranded here, too." he observed.

Janene did not reply to his obvious assessment of her situation. He left her striding arrogantly toward a nearby phone booth. Immediately, she dismissed him from her thoughts and re-established herself on her luggage perch. However, it was uncomfortable so she stood again contemplating miserably the long wait ahead of her.

As there was no one around, she walked across the

short distance to the darkened waiting room. She tried the sliding gate to the closed off area to find it locked. 'How inconsiderate', she thought crossly. 'They might have left the area open. It would certainly be more comfortable to recline in one of those leather chairs for a five hour wait.' She returned to her suitcase wishing only for a comfortable place to sit down. She gathered up her belongings, found an empty storage locker, and bestowed all but her shoulder bag inside, then carefully removed the key to place it in her bag. She had just finished her task when the same husky voice brought her to attention.

"I've just called my chauffeur to fetch me. Why don't you allow me to drive you home?" She turned startled wide blue eyes toward the speaker. She surveyed him critically for a brief moment, taking in the breadth and height of him as his steel grey eyes locked with hers. "It's not that far out of our way," he continued. "My home is in Brea. The chauffeur will be here in approximately an hour. We'll drive you straight to your apartment and you'll be saved a very long wait , to say nothing of the long ride after that." She was aware of the amused expression that flickered across his eyes and threatened the corners of his firm lips. "No strings attached," he added softly.

"Thanks, but no thanks," she answered coolly, turning abruptly away from him. The hand on her elbow was light but she was instantly aware of the virile magnetism of the man. His fingers seemed to electrify her whole body. Quickly she withdrew from his searing touch.

"Suit yourself," he said with dry amusement.

"However, I think you're cutting off your nose to spite your face."

"Is that so?" she snapped.

"I suppose you think I should jump at the chance of riding into the night with an absolute stranger."

"No, on the contrary. Believe it or not, I can appreciate you hesitation. However, we are caught in a set of rather unusual circumstances. There is no way out of here this morning without a long wait for the airport limousine. I've already tried to secure a taxi and they won't accept a run of that distance in this fog. That is why I called my home and ordered my chauffeur to come and get me. I, for one don't intend to spend the remainder of the night waiting here for some transportation out of this place."

"Do you really have a chauffeur?" she asked suddenly. He smiled openly this time. Despite herself, Janene smiled back. She heard the throaty chuckle escape as he smiled indulgently at her.

"Did you think I was making it up?" he asked quietly.

"Yes," she said honestly. "I'm still not convinced."

"Suppose we go have some breakfast or at least coffee and I'll try to convince you," he challenged. Again Janene hesitated.

"I can't possibly ravish you in a place like this." he teased, amusement causing his grey eyes to twinkle wickedly.

"All right," Janene replied. His light touch was at her elbow again guiding her down the corridor toward the neon sign that marked the entrance to the coffee shop. Janene was surprised to find upon entering that the coffee shop was nearly full. He guided her deftly to a booth and they sat down.

"What will you have?" he asked.

"Just coffee, please," she answered coyly.

"Sure you won't have breakfast? I'm starved."

She shook her head. She was hungry but she knew instinctively that he would insist upon paying for anything she might order and she didn't want to be indebted in any way to this handsome stranger.

"You're sure you don't want something to eat?" he asked lightly as he gave his order for steak and eggs to the waitress.

Janene shook her head. "Make that two orders," he added ignoring her shaking head.

"Why did you do that?" Janene asked sharply when the waitress had departed. "I told you I wasn't hungry."

"So you did," he replied. "But it doesn't take a crystal ball to see that you are tired and food is a known restorer of energy. Besides, I'm hungry enough that I can probably eat yours, too, if you find you really can't eat it." He offered her a cigarette which she accepted with murmured thanks. As he lit the cigarette for her, holding the lighter towards her, their eyes met. "Relax," he urged. "I don't eat tired, stranded females, even lovely ones, at least not on sight," he teased. Janene smiled, allowing herself to settle more comfortably into the booth seat as she drew on her cigarette veiling her eyes with the exhaled smoke. Their coffee arrived and its warmth revived Janene somewhat. She found herself reconsidering his offer of a lift home although earlier she had resolved not to put herself into any such situation. She was innately cautious having only recently moved into the metropolitan atmosphere from the small town country life in which she had been raised. She wasn't really afraid just considered it wiser to have complete control of any situation in which she became involved. Silently she considered the pros and cons of the stranger's proposal.

"Have you arrived at a decision?" he asked minutes later.

"Regarding what?" she countered being deliberately obtuse. He did not reply but rather continued on a different vein.

"My name is Vance Reeves. I've been in San Francisco on business. I usually fly myself as I have my own plane but this time of year I tend to rely on public transportation. I own a fairly lucrative estate not far from Brea. I called there after first speaking to you and asked the family chauffeur to bring the car here to retrieve me and run me home. As I mentioned earlier, he will be arriving shortly. I'm perfectly willing to drive you to Santa Ana or anywhere else in the nearby area. I hate having to wait myself and rather gathered you might feel similarly. You may consider it my good deed for the day."

Janene sensed he was laughing at her which did little to appease her anxious reluctance. She really wanted to get home and have some sleep but she couldn't quite decide if the man before her was for real. Nevertheless, she had to admit that if this was a line to cajole her into accompanying him for whatever purpose he might have in mind, it was certainly original. She didn't consider herself so blatantly attractive that he should attempt to pick her up for a night's diversion particularly with the night nearly gone. Still her cautious nature made her hesitant, unduly quiet.

As if he had been reading her mind, he spoke between a couple of bites of steak. So far, she had not touched her plate.

"Eat up." he urged. "then we'll get out of here. I'm not a white slave trader and I promise not to compromise you in any way. I meant it when I said no strings attached. I just hate to see you waiting around here until morning when in a short time you can be home and in what I hope might be more comfortable surroundings."

Janene nodded without making further comment and proceeded to eat. The food was good and Janene discovered with embarrassment that she was attacking it with gusto. She looked up to find Vance Reeves watching her and nearly choked on the bites she had taken. She blushed as her eyes met his. He signaled the waitress for more coffee. When the waitress had refilled their cups and departed, Janene murmured softly.

"This is good. I was hungrier than I thought."

He nodded. "I rather thought you might be. I considered it likely that you weren't exactly overjoyed at the prospect of my buying you breakfast. We can make it Dutch treat if that makes you feel better though I assure you it isn't necessary. I, also, dislike dining alone and despite the fact you have been unduly quiet I've enjoyed the company.

Thank-you," Janene demurred. "I'm truly sorry. I guess I have been behaving a little silly.

"On the contrary," he contradicted. "I find your attitude refreshing. There aren't many young women today who hesitate to take all they can from any man who offers, much less hesitate being picked up. Tell me about yourself."

"There's not much to tell," Janene smiled warmly. "I'm just a small town girl whose career has taken her into the cosmopolitan scene to earn a living."

"I see," he commented not pressing for further details. They finished their breakfast lingering over coffee. They didn't talk a great deal but the silence between them was not an uncomfortable one. It was rather a natural phenomenon as it was apparent to them both how tired each was. Presently, Vance arose to pay the bill and when he returned to the table a few minutes later, another man accompanied him. His companion was dressed in a blue serge uniform and carried a chauffeur's cap. "Janene," Vance spoke quietly. "Charles is here, are you ready to go?" Janene nodded and stood up. Vance took her elbow, lightly propelling her toward the door. Once again, her reluctance betrayed itself, his fingers tightened slightly. "It's all right," Vance urged softly then, "Give me your key and I'll have Charles get your things."

Until that moment, Janene had not realized that he carried no luggage only a brief case which he'd kept with him constantly. She found herself wondering what his business was and chided herself for neglecting to ask him. Again his perceptiveness unnerved her as he casually took her luggage locker key from trembling fingers which he clasped firmly in his hand, transferring the key to Charles with clipped instructions. As the chauffeur left to retrieve her belongings, he looked down at her steadily. "I flew to San Francisco early this morning before the fog had settled in so I haven't any luggage. Under normal conditions, I should have been home hours ago. In case you haven't noticed, I need a shave," he added taking her hand which he still held to rub it against his cheek. She felt the rough stubble that was beginning to form. He did not release her hand but dropped them both to his side between them. Abruptly Janene relaxed and he smiled at her.

Whatever she was letting herself in for at that instant she no longer cared. For some reason she had a sudden complete faith in the man at her side and relaxed fingers clasped gently within the grasp of his had communicated her feelings to him. Charles led the way to the parked car, a sleek black Rolls Royce. He stowed the luggage in the rear compartment as Vance helped Janene into the roomy back seat and lowered his lean length onto the seat beside her. Janene adjusted the slim skirt of her black traveling suit and relaxed wearily against the soft cushions. Charles slid under the wheel and ignited the car's motor. The huge automobile moved effortlessly away from the curb. They were well on the way down the highway and had emerged onto the Santa Ana Freeway southward when Vance spoke softly, his breath warm against her ear.

"Have you fallen asleep already, princess?" he asked.

"No," came Janene's quick answer as she straightened moving away from him. She could sense he was amused by her coolness but she was uncaring. He, too, had straightened away from her and when he spoke again although his voice was still quietly low, she knew he was facing straight ahead.

"Then, don't you think you had better tell me your address so I can inform Charles where we are headed?" he chuckled and she could almost see the wicked gleam in his eyes through the blackness as he added, "otherwise, he may just assume you plan to share the same roof with me for the rest of the night, more precisely the same bed."

Hastily, Janene gave him her address. He, in turn, leaned forward to repeat the address to Charles along with some other instructions which she could not hear. Janene had turned her face toward the side window. She could see nothing. The fog was dense and even the freeway guide lights remained invisible until they were nearly upon them. Abruptly the huge car halted veering sharply as its driver braked then fought for control to avoid colliding with the tail lights of the vehicle ahead. Janene was thrown roughly forward. She collided with Vance's shoulder and outstretched arm as the abrupt stop hurled her ahead. She realized Vance had seen the tail lights almost as soon as his driver and had deliberately braced himself to break her collision with the front seat. His hand clasped her far shoulder firmly, his arm pressed tightly against her breasts. Although they could not have been traveling fast the car skidded as it halted. For a full moment Vance held her firmly against him then eased her back against the cushions moving with her.

"Are you all right?" he asked brusquely.

"Yes," she replied breathlessly partly due to the jolt and partly due to his nearness.

"What is it, Charles?" he demanded.

"I don't know, Mr. Vance," came the somber reply. "Traffic is apparently halted for some reason. Is everything all right back there?"

"Fine, Charles, we're okay." Vance settled back on the seat beside Janene and proceeded to light a cigarette. She sensed his impatience at the unknown delay as his body was rigidly alert. After several minutes, he leaned forward again resting on the front seat back as he spoke urgently to Charles. The two men talked quietly in subdued tones. Janene didn't try to distinguish their words. Without a word to her, Vance opened the door and climbed out. Janene shivered as the damp January air rushed into the car and pulled her jacket more securely about her. Fervently, she wished she had not packed her coat in the suitcase, however, much she detested traveling in a bulky coat. Vance was gone for a long time. Janene had kicked off her shoes and was curled up in the seat. The chauffeur had shut off the motor shortly after Vance's departure from the car and damp chill had settled over its interior. 'What a revolting development', she thought slightly irritated at herself for agreeing to Vance's suggestion to take her home. At least the airport terminal had been warm.

Charles' voice interrupted her reverie. "Are you cold, miss?" he inquired solicitously.

"A little," she admitted.

"Do you wish me to start the engine?"

"Oh, no, don't do that," she replied. "I should have taken my coat out of my suitcase, I guess," she added thinking aloud.

"I can get it for you if you like, Miss," Charles offered immediately.

"No, I'm sure we won't be here that long. There's no need for you to bother but thank you."

"I'm not so sure, Miss. Mr. Vance has been gone quite awhile. It's really no bother either." With that he started out of the car. She could hear him removing her case from the boot and in a few seconds the door beside her opened. "Here you are, Miss." he said placing the suitcase on the roadway. She stepped out, opened her case and took the long tan camel's hair coat from it. Charles closed the case and was already returning it to the boot by the time she had wrapped the coat securely about her chilled frame and returned to the softness of the car seat. Another ten minutes passed before Vance returned. He climbed into the car rubbing his hands briskly together.

"Damn, but it's cold out there," he complained as he settled into the seat. Janene uncurled her body and was searching with her bare feet for her shoes when she felt his arm slip behind her and his hand at her waist as he drew her back against him. "Don't be such a selfish little minx," he scolded. "I'm cold and I don't have a warm coat to snuggle into. Besides it's more fun to snuggle close to you," he whispered teasingly. Gradually Janene relaxed against his shoulder. She could feel the warm length of his body stirring her senses as he snuggled her closer to him.

"That's better," he murmured against her hair before adding, "You smell good." He nibbled delicately at her ear lobe, gently touching her with his soft, moist lips. His actions sent pleasant messages along her spine. Janene stiffened and tried unsuccessfully to pull away. She turned her head slightly as his hand cupped her chin turning her face upward toward his own. His lips covered her open mouth as she started to speak. Sensuously, experimentally his lips pressed hers, exploring her mouth and evoking the shuddering response she wasn't prepared to give. As his passion rose, flared by her own sudden response, his kiss became more persuasive and demanding. Then suddenly he released her lips, but his arms still held her firmly. Unable to move away and not all certain that she wanted to, Janene buried her head against his shoulder. The rapid beating of his heart pounded in her ears as she sought to regain control of her errant emotions. His arms relaxed and reluctantly she moved, conscious of his closeness and the feel of his left arm still encircling her shoulders lightly. Slowly, he withdrew that, too, and lit a cigarette. He offered it to her silently. She took the cigarette and drew deeply allowing the smoke to escape wispily from her nostrils. He lit another for himself. He drew deeply and exhaled before his husky voice broke the tense silence.

"I'm not going to apologize for that, Janene. I've felt like kissing you ever since I first saw you sitting so forlornly on your suitcase at the airport. I'm just sorry my timing is so damn clumsy." Janene moved away from him to the far side of the seat not trusting herself to speak. Her feet had found her pumps and she sat sedately on her side of the car.

"Are you frightened?" he asked softly.

"No," she replied in a tight voice. "A little puzzled, I guess but not scared."

"Good girl," he said. "I promise it won't happen again, okay?"

"Okay," she agreed readily though she was vaguely disappointed. Quickly she chided herself for her foolish thoughts. Lord, she hardly knew the man and yet he had stirred with in her emotions she thought nonexistent.

"I'm still cold, he teased.

She giggled nervously before asking, "And what do you suggest I do about that?" She wondered if he was smiling at her and wished she could see his face.

"You could snuggle up to me, again," he chuckled.

"I think I'll pass for the moment," she retorted lightly.

"Okay, if that's how you're going to be, I guess I'll have to find someone or something else to warm me up. Somehow, I don't think Charles will fulfill the requirements." He opened a small compartment attached to the back of the front seat. To Janene's amazement a small table descended to display hidden behind it a well-equipped bar. She could not conceal her curiosity, for never before, except in movies, had she seen anything like this.

"Would you care for a brandy?" he asked. Janene shook her head, then realizing he could not see her through the darkness of the car despite the dim light that illuminated the bar's contents said no. He ignored her answer and carefully extracted two glasses, pouring a small amount of amber liquid into each and extending one toward her.

She took it hesitantly. "Come on, sip it," he urged. "It won't weaken your defenses that much and I did promise, didn't I?" He continued persuasively. She took a tiny sip discovering that it wasn't nearly as strong as she had anticipated and that it did feel warming to her chilled body.

"What's happening out there?" she asked.

"There's been a rather nasty accident some distance ahead. I didn't learn any specific details but evidently someone is quite badly hurt. At any rate it may take some time to clear it away and re-open the highway." He paused thoughtfully sipping his brandy. "I'm sorry, princess. Perhaps you would have been wiser not to have accepted my offer to drive you home. Doesn't look like you'll be home much faster anyway. I'm really sorry," he continued.

"It's all right, Vance. You couldn't have known this would happen. Besides, it has been an experience so far. In more ways than one," she added with a giggle, choking on the sip of brandy she had taken. He patted her rather roughly on the back as she coughed, then intimately slipped his arm about her, drawing her against him as he settled back against the firm seat. This time she offered no resistance but relaxed comfortably within the cozy circle of his arm. Neither spoke as they sat sipping their drinks. Janene found she was growing increasingly tired. She yawned sleepily. Vance took the glass from her and replaced both his and hers in the bar cupboard and closed the compartment.

Then pulling her closer into the circle of his arm, he whispered, "Go to sleep, kitten, at least it's fairly comfortable here."

Janene had not realized, until she felt the cold damp night air, that Charles had left the car. As he slid beneath the wheel she snuggled deeper in Vance's protective arm and felt him tighten his hold while shifting his body to draw her even nearer.

Charles turned toward the rear seat saying, "Mr. Vance, they said it will be at least another hour before the road is cleared for through traffic. Should we continue to wait? I can inch ahead to the exit and drive on in to Brea. We're only a few miles from home. The young lady can rest there until the fog lifts and I can run her home then."

"What do you say, kitten?" Vance whispered against the top of her head. "Your place or mine?"

"I don't care," Janene murmured sleepily, her eyes closing drowsily. "Go, ahead, Charles. See if you can get us home. I'm beat and the lady is thoroughly exhausted."

# Chapter 2

Charles started the car and inched it forward around the parked vehicles. Vaguely aware they were moving but uncaringly, Janene dozed then slept in the arm of her stranger.

When Janene awakened she sat up startled and confused by the unfamiliar surroundings. Everything was strange. The room was large. A fireplace still glowing with dying embers occupied one end of the room. Before it sat two massive leather chairs. An enormous chest occupied one wall and the king-sized four poster upon which she lay completely filled its end of the room. It was quite obviously a man's room. Panically, she allowed her gaze to drift to the other side of the bed half expecting to see the indentation upon the pillow that would indicate she had not slept alone. She sighed with relief when the rest of the bed appeared unmussed and evidently unused. A faint smell of men's cologne clung to the room, tickling her quivering nostrils. Her clothes were hung or rather slung over the arm of one of the leather chairs. Blushingly, she realized that she wore nothing but the bed clothes. She lay back against the pillow disturbed, her mind whirled as she sought to recall what, why and how she came to be in this room, in this bed.

Slowly, her dazed mind cleared and she remembered the flight to Ontario and the bus ride into the Los Angeles terminal. Gradually her memory produced Vance Reeves and her reluctant acceptance of a ride to her apartment. Finally, the accident and their delay on the highway was recalled. No amount of prodding, however, seemed to reveal how she came to be sleeping in a strange bed in a totally unfamiliar room. Logic told her the room must belong to Vance but if so why was she here. She glanced at her watch. It read three o'clock. Morning or afternoon?' she wondered absently. 'It must be afternoon', she concluded thoughtfully. 'After all it had been well past two when they had left the airport in Reeves' limousine.'

A sudden warmth engulfed her as she remembered Vance's kiss and her willing response. This must be his place in Brea, but when had she entered this room and why was she here now? She had just decided to crawl out of bed, when a sharp rap at the door sent her scurrying back into the confines of the bed covers. She had barely concealed her nakedness beneath the blankets when the door opened quietly and a tall male figure strode into the room.

"So you're finally awake are you, kitten," he drawled as he came to stand beside the bed, his grey eyes looking down at her.

"It would appear so," she snapped pulling the covers more tightly under her chin.

"Well, are you going to stay there snuggled up like at Eskimo forever?" he inquired with a sly grin.

"I am as long as you remain standing there," she retorted testily.

"Is that so, why?" he teased impishly. "I've seen women in their night clothes before. Come on, hop out," he added grabbing the covers quickly and giving them a sharp tug. Janene held them securely.

"You know damn well I haven't anything on and don't you dare yank on those blankets again." she threatened weakly.

"Oh," he grinned wickedly. He tugged lightly at the covers again. She clutched them frantically.

"Vance Reeves, get out of here immediately or I'll scream bloody murder," she threatened more sharply.

"And just what good do you think that will do? You're in my room and in my bed to say nothing of the fact that there is no one else in the house."

For a moment, Janene felt real terror. Her eyes widened, she stared at Vance indecisively. His gaze locked with her own momentarily then he laughed. Thoroughly annoyed, she glared at him knowing he was merely having fun at her expense and in no way appreciating his suggestive humor.

"You're a devil," she snorted hotly. " Now get out of here so I can get up and get dressed. By the way why am I here in the first place?"

"All in due time my pet," he crooned dropping lazily down beside her to lie full length at her side.

"Vance, will you please get out of here," she pleaded. "What will people say?"

"Well," he drawled lazily. "I imagine they would think I've been making violent, passionate love to you though I really should shed some clothes first." He reached for the buckle of his belt and began to loosen it. Then suddenly he rolled over, flopped an arm across her prone body and covered her lips gently with his own. He released her just as quickly and sprang to his feet. "All right, kitten, I'll quit teasing you. I'll leave but only if you promise to join me for breakfast in one half hour. By the way your suitcase is in the dressing room," he gestured toward a second doorway leading from the room. "There's a shower, towels etc. Would you like me to stay and scrub your back?" he grinned wickedly.

"No, I would not," she snapped, grabbing the pillow beside her and sitting up to fling it violently at him. He caught it deftly, clutching it against his chest. His dark hair still damp from his own recent shower curled rakishly over his forehead. His eyes danced mischievously as he peered over the pillow back at her. The sheet Janene clutched had slipped exposing the rounded upper curvature and slight cleavage of her bare breasts, with her effort to expose her arm and fling the pillow at him. She followed the line of his gaze feeling the color rising to her cheeks and pulled the sheet higher.

"Let that sheet slip a little more and I might decide I don't want to leave after all," he taunted. Blushingly, she settled back into the cover depths.

"Just get out of here you, cad," she spat angrily.

"I'm going," he insisted making little move to do so. Then wickedly he added. "I think I'd have more fun here than in the kitchen though." With an implicating look and a sly wink he left the room closing the door behind him. For a few moments, Janene remained where she was not at all certain he had really gone. Finally, she slid from the bed pulling the spread with her and using it as a robe.

She made her way to the adjoining dressing room. She passed through the room noting the masculine toiletries and turned on the shower in the connecting bathroom.

Once under the shower she tensed remembering she had locked none of the doors. There was nothing to prevent Vance from wandering in on her. Deliberately, she abandoned her apprehension and without haste showered and dressed. She chose a pair of navy slacks and a white turtle-neck sweater, emerging some thirty minutes later her hair damp but groomed and her makeup carefully applied. She felt and knew she looked refreshed. She was tall, nearly five foot eight. She wore little make-up, just lipstick and mascara. Her golden hair glistened and shone with cleanliness. Regaining some of her confidence she slipped stockinged feet into black flats and surveyed herself in the mirror critically. Not seeing herself as particularly attractive, she satisfied herself that she looked reasonably presentable. She missed the rose pink tinge of her cheeks and the sparkling luster of her blue eyes. She was about to turn away from the mirror when she saw from the corner of her eye the door open and Vance enter. Pretending a calm she in no way felt, she adjusted the turtle-neck of her sweater.

"Don't you ever knock?" she inquired testily.

"Not usually upon my own bedroom door," he returned with a smile. His eyes traveled rakishly over her slim figure giving her the distinct feeling that he was deliberately disrobing her in his mind. She ignored the look deciding it was better to let well enough alone. He had far too much effect upon her senses as it was. She certainly didn't want him to know it embarrassed her to think he had been responsible for undressing and putting her to bed earlier. Nevertheless, she felt herself begin to flush slightly at his intentionally admiring gaze. She had the distinct impression he knew exactly where her thoughts lie.

Quickly she moved across the room gathering up the strewn clothes and replacing the bedspread. She knew he leaned lazily against the now closed door watching her. Unable to bear his scrutiny any longer, she plumped everything upon the bed and turned to face him. She had not heard him move across the carpeted floor and bumped smack against him as she turned. His arms encircled her lightly as she lifted her head to look. A queer feeling swept through her veins, their eyes met and held. He had shaved, the heady scent of his cologne plus his nearness unsettled her equilibrium and she swayed unconsciously toward him. His moist lips parted of their own volition. He stared down at her tenderly, then lowered his head as his lips met hers. With a groan he drew her closer. Devouring her mouth tenderly at first, then with growing passion, his lips evoking the response in her that he sought. She stiffened as his hands slipped beneath her sweater and she felt the pressure of his warm palm against her bare flesh. He released her and stepped away from her. His arms falling limply to his sides.

"I know," he said gruffly "I promised not to do that again, but I don't seem to be able to stop myself. You don't help much either. I get the distinct message you're not nearly so unmoved as you say." His eyes sought hers and she suddenly realized he too was confused by the electrifying current that flared between them. She met his gaze steadily, ignoring his question but with a smile saying. "Didn't you say something about food?"

"That I did, kitten," he replied accepting her cue. "That's why I came upstairs in the first place, to see if you were ready to eat. Come, on," he added clasping her hand lightly and pulling her after him as he strode purposefully toward the door. As they descended the stairs, the aroma of freshly brewed coffee and frying bacon tantalized her nostrils.

Janene realized how utterly famished she was. "I'm starved," she commented, adding, "It sure smells good." He smiled at her warmly as he led her into the dining room. The table was set for two. Vance held her chair then seated himself opposite her. She immediately drank of the deliciously cooled orange juice in her glass. She was surprised a moment later when the door opened and a matronly grey-haired woman entered bearing a tray laden with eggs, bacon and hot biscuits which she smilingly placed before them on the table. The woman retreated, only to return once more with a steaming pot of coffee. She poured the coffee filling two cups, pausing beside Janene.

"Did you rest well, Miss? You certainly look more refreshed than you did last night or I guess it was this morning," she chuckled. "Doesn't she, Mr. Vance?"

"That she does, Dora," Vance agreed. Janene looked from one to the other puzzled.

"You were more than half asleep when Mr. Vance

carried you upstairs last night. I thought I was never going to get you into bed. But, I'm glad you're looking rested this afternoon," the woman rattled continuously.

"Thank you," Janene murmured. "I slept very well." She glanced at Vance. His eyes, twinkling with amusement, met hers across the table. Annoyed at him she couldn't keep the flush from creeping into her cheeks as she dropped her eyes. Dora left the room but Janene stubbornly refused to look up from her plate. She helped herself to the tray Vance slid toward her concentrating intently upon her food. A throaty chuckle from the man across from her brought her head up with a start. Her eyes met his. He was smiling broadly and for an instant she felt like throwing her plate and its contents at him. Instead, she smiled then joined in his laughter.

"You're a louse," she said indignantly though her own laughter tranquilized the sarcastic sting of her words.

"Why?" he asked innocently, amusement still twitching at the corners of his mouth while he tried to don a somber expression.

"You know damn well, why," she retorted.

"A lady shouldn't swear, darling. Whatever will poor Dora think?" he chuckled. "Besides I haven't the slightest idea what you're talking about. What is it I'm accused of doing now?"

"You deliberately let me think we were alone in the house and furthermore," her voice faltered as she hesitated to put the rest of her thoughts into words.

"And furthermore you thought I was the one who had undressed and put you to bed this morning. Did you, also, check to see if you had slept alone when you awakened?"

"As a matter of fact I did," Janene agreed.

"Did you wish I had?" he asked softly.

"What?" she inquired warily.

"Put you to bed and slept beside you, with you or whatever," he prompted.

"No, I did not," she replied testily.

"Well, I wish I had. I'm not usually so easily deterred from a direct course?"

"You're insufferable," she snapped hotly embarrassed. "But at least you are honest, no wonder neither your chauffeur nor your housekeeper blink an eye when you show up with a strange woman in tow. It's probably a regular occurrence. I'm just glad you had a shred of decency left."

"The lady doth protest too much me thinks," Vance drawled tauntingly.

"Oh, just shut up." Janene flared raising the coffee cup to her lips to sip the hot liquid. There was a pronounced silence for several minutes as they ate. Dora reappeared to refill the coffee cups. Their appetites satiated, Vance slid his chair back slightly and produced a pack of cigarettes. He offered Janene one but she refused, content to drink her coffee. She rarely smoked anyway. Finally, she stood up, taking her cup of coffee with her. She crossed to the drapery covered windows and began searching for the pull string. Vance reached around her and pulled open the drapes.

# Chapter 3

The fog had not lifted. It's heavy blanket covered everything in bleak greyness. "It's still awfully foggy out there," she said unnecessarily.

He nodded. "Yes, it's been causing all sorts of traffic problems. According to the radio it is even denser toward the coast."

"Can Charles take me home do you think?" she asked soberly.

"I suppose it's possible to get through but it is not going to be easy. Do you have to get back?"

"Not really. I don't have to be to work until the tenth. Today's the seventh, right? I would like to get home though." she added.

"Stay here with me until the fog lifts," he urged softly. "I don't know, Vance. I don't think that is such a good idea. Besides it isn't exactly fair. I don't want to put you to all that trouble. Perhaps, I can get a taxi."

"It's no trouble. I'd like you to stay. Charles and I will run you into Santa Anna if you insist upon going but what is the point. Driving anywhere in this weather is hazardous. You said you really don't have to get back for a few days. There's plenty of room."

"But I'm in your bedroom," she complained.

"So you are but I can't really see that it is a disadvantage," he teased. "In fact, it is rather a decided advantage from my point of view," Catching the fleeting apprehension in her eyes, his voice changed tone and he added seriously.

"You are perfectly safe, Janene, I won't press my attentions upon you. I won't do anything you don't want me to do. As for the fact you are in my bedroom, it was easier to deposit you there this morning so you could rest rather than trying to awaken you sufficiently enough for Dora to prepare the guest room. So I made it up while Dora was putting you to bed and I slept in there. You're welcome to my room for a couple of nights."

"What time is it?" Janene asked.

"About five." Vance answered glancing at the gold watch he wore upon his wrist.

"I don't suppose there is much chance it will lift tonight?" she mused absently.

"I doubt it but let's see if we can catch some news and a weather report," he suggested turning toward the hallway. Janene followed him. He led the way to another room which Janene decided was a den. A fire blazed in the white brick fireplace invitingly. Before it stretched a long, black leather couch flanked on either side by large matching leather chairs. One side of the room was encased with a full wall bookcase lined with books. Opposite black drapes hid what was probably a large picture window. Before it stood a massive desk and swivel chair. A colored television set sat at the end of the fireplace in the corner of the room. It was to this that Vance strode. Switching it on, he flipped the dial until a news cast program became visible. He then lowered his tall frame into one of the leather chairs and was soon intently absorbed in the screen. Janene closed the door and crossed toward the fireplace. She stood before it sipping her coffee which had become lukewarm, distastefully. "Would you like some more coffee?" he asked as he caught the distasteful grimace on her face. "That has to be cold and besides I could do with another cup."

"I'll get it," she offered but found it unnecessary for Dora entered at that moment carrying a tray.

"Thank you, Dora" Vance accepted. He took Janene's cup and refilled it then filled another cup for himself. It became apparent to Janene, as she listened watching the news broadcast, that insisting on traveling in the heavy fog would be foolish. This conclusion to herself, however, did not relieve her inner tension. She was intensely aware of the man lounging casually across the room from her. She studied his rugged handsome features as he sat engrossed in the program. His forehead was high. Thick dark brown eyebrows lined deep set eyes. His aquiline nose was a bit too long but was offset by full sensuous lips. The squarish jawline led to a firm strong chin. His shoulders were broad and though encased in a black turtle-necked sweater, Janene could see the lean, rippling, muscular strength of his chest. Over six feet, his slim hips and muscular thighs strained against the form fitting black pants he wore. She could almost visualize a black Stetson upon his head and gun-belt strapped to his narrow flat waist. He reminded her of the stereotyped gunfighter often pictured in old-time Western movies. She had little doubt that the steel grey eyes could turn cold as ice, the lips press into a firm, even cruel smile if he so desired. His virile masculinity permeated the room and she silently admitted that she was deeply attracted to him. She deliberately shrugged off the thought as a queer result of physical chemistry.

At twenty six she had had her fair share of light romances. Had even thought herself in love once or twice but total commitment had not been for her. In recent years, she had accepted her life as it was and she wasn't sure she ever wanted a serious involvement with any man. Vance would demand complete submission from his women. There would be no equality of the sexes with a man like him. She didn't want to remain in close proximity with Vance Reeves even for just a few days. Janene was not a prude but neither did she sleep around. Vance had already shown his interest in her. She felt uneasy, vulnerable. It would not do to delude herself into believing that Vance's interest meant anything lasting. To allow herself to fall in love with the man would spell certain heartache. That was one thing she didn't need right now.

A sigh escaped her lips and at the same moment, she realized that Vance was looking at her. She met his gaze briefly then turned to face the glowing firelight.

"What's the matter, kitten? he asked.

"Nothing, " she replied. "I was just wishing the fog would lift. It is so depressing."

"Does that mean you are already bored with my company?" Vance inquired sardonically.

"No, I didn't mean that," she answered a little too hastily. "I guess I'm a little restless."

She moved to the bookcase and began reading

some of the titles. It was an amazing collection. She found herself wondering if Vance had read all of them. Many of the titles were histories of the old West; there was a complete collection of the works of Zane Grey and B. M. Bower. There were, also, books on silver and gold mines, early California and the Southwest. There were even a few of Louis Lamour's more modern westerns. There were many of the classics including a complete set of Shakespearean works, and several Dicken's selections.

Janene browsed interestedly, oblivious to all else. Vance's voice at her side startled her. "Do you enjoy reading?" he asked.

She nodded wordlessly.

"So do I," he continued. " I've read most of these at one time or another. Help yourself if you see anything you like."

"Thank you," she replied simply. She continued to drift aimlessly among the shelves, pausing now and then to read a title more thoroughly. When she eventually turned away from the shelves the room was empty. She walked slowly back to the fireplace then curled up in the chair Vance had recently vacated. She was soon immersed in watching the old Andy Hardy movie showing on the television. Sometime later, she heard Vance return. He added some logs

"Have you decided to stay with me?" he asked as the movie concluded.

She nodded. "I can't ask you or Charles to risk an accident by driving home. I'll stay until the fog lifts. Thank you."

"Janene, I want you to feel free to move about the house and do whatever you like. Would you like to take a tour of the place?"

"I'd rather do that in the day light," she answered yawning lazily.

"Are you tired?"

"Not really." She'd looked at him smiling. "I'm just lazy, you don't have to entertain me, Vance."

"Right, I've some paper work to do." He handed her the television remote control mechanism and was soon settled behind the massive desk. "Won't the television bother you?" she asked.

"No I always have it on when I work in here. It keeps me company."

She watched television for awhile then dozed. She was awakened by a delicate brush of lips against hers. She groaned and stretched, eyes remaining closed.

"Don't do that," he whispered, "or I really will kiss you awake." She sat up quickly to find her arms entwined about Vance's neck. "I'm sorry," she stammered. "I guess I was dreaming."

"It must have been some dream," he quipped. " I rather like believing you knew it was me," he teased soberly. "It's after nine, are you hungry?"

"A little," she admitted. "Good. Dora has made some sandwiches, etc. Shall we eat here by the fire?"

"Yes, let's but first I'd like to wash up."

"Fine, I will tell Dora to bring things in here while you do just that." Janene bounded up the stairs.

In a few minutes she returned to find Vance waiting

before the fire. They ate turkey sandwiches washed down with hot coffee in silence. The tray sitting on the couch in front of them. It was a comfortable silence and Janene felt fully relaxed for the first time all evening.

When they had finished Dora came in and removed the remains informing them that she was retiring soon.

"Goodnight, Dora," Vance called as the woman left the room. He fixed them a drink and returned to sit beside Janene on the couch. Though they were not touching, Janene's senses were keenly alerted to his nearness. She searched desperately for an excuse to retire herself, but the problem was she really wasn't sleepy. She strongly suspected Vance would see through any excuse she might perpetrate.

"Do you type?" Vance asked suddenly.

"Yes, I'm quite good at it. Why?"

"Well, I have some letters to get off and I thought perhaps if the fog hasn't lifted by morning, you might be willing to give me a hand with them," Vance confessed. "Suppose it's too much to hope for that you take shorthand," he drawled lazily.

"As a matter of fact, I do take shorthand but I'm not very fast," she answered.

"We'll manage," he prophesied, slipping his arm behind her and allowing it to fall lightly along her shoulders. She started to resist but thought better of it. He drew her closer and she snuggled against his shoulder just as she had done the night before in the car. They sat watching the fire blaze warmly. Presently Vance stirred tightening his arm and turning her toward him.

"No, Vance, don't," she murmured softly.

"Don't you want me to kiss you?"

"No, yes, I don't know," she stammered completely flustered.

"I want to kiss you," he said bluntly. "I like holding you in my arms." She looked up at him, unaware of the tenderness lighting her eyes. His eyes held hers briefly before he bent his head to kiss her gently. Of their own volition her arms stole about his neck and she gave herself over to the thrill and ecstasy his lips provided. He seemed to draw her even nearer, the pressure of his lips becoming more demanding.

He lifted his head briefly to gaze at her intently. Then his lips sent a trail of fire as he moved them lightly across her throat and recaptured her lips. He lowered her carefully back against the cushions half covering her body with his own. His hand slipped beneath her sweater and she felt the warm pressure against bare flesh. She turned her head away pushing gently against his chest with both her palms.

His free hand moved beneath her sweater to touch the curve of her breast sending a quiver of delight through her entire body. As he released the catch of her bra, she stiffened and violently pushed him away.

"What is it with you anyway?" he said gruffly, regaining his balance as she pulled herself into a sitting position. "What the hell kind of game are you playing or are you just a tease? Everything's fine up to a point then you grow cold and prudish."

"I'm sorry," she answered softly.

"Sorry, hell, I don't buy it."

It's just that I intend to sleep alone tonight." she snapped coldly.

"Did I suggest otherwise?" he mocked quietly.

"Not in so many words, no, but that's where all this is leading isn't it? That's what you've had in mind every since you first decided to offer me a ride home. No strings attached I believe you said. What a laugh! Just a romp in the hay and then I can go my merry way. You disgust me. If you don't mind, I think I'd like to go upstairs now."

She stood up, reaching behind herself to re-snap her unhooked bra, her eyes glaring at him. He sat calmly relaxed, watching her. She turned sharply away but a strong hand clasped her wrist in a vice-like grip.

"But, I do mind, Kitten," he crooned softly forcing her to sit down beside him. "What are you afraid of?" he queried. "Me or yourself?"

She turned away from his intent gaze. "I told you before that nothing would happen that you didn't want to happen." He paused to let his words sink in before continuing, " You weren't exactly pushing me away you know. In case it has escaped your notice, it takes two to make love. I'm not so far gone that I have to force myself on any woman." His voice had grown cold, hard with barely controlled anger. Abruptly he released her wrist and stood up. He lit a cigarette and puffed on it in strained silence.

Janene leaned back against the cushions rubbing her wrist free of the pain his tight grip had caused.

"Have you ever been in love, Janene?" he asked huskily after minutes had ticked by.

"No, I don't think I really have. I thought I was in love a couple of times but it didn't work out. After awhile I wasn't even sorry the relationship had ended."

"Well, I have and believe me it is not all it's cracked up to be. It hurts like hell and I swore I'd never let any woman get that kind of hold on me again, ever! I'm no monk but I'm no sex maniac either."

"What happened to her?" Janene asked softly beginning to understand the hidden depths hiding within her handsome stranger.

"The usual, I found her in bed with another man. He just happened to by my best friend at the time. They were both visiting in my home for the weekend. It was to have been the weekend of our engagement party. I threw them both out, lock stock and barrel."

"How awful for you," Janene murmured.

"Not for me. I'm just glad that I found out what a tramp she was before I married her. She was a tease like you. She kept me at arms length holding out for that damn wedding ring while she hopped in bed with every Tom, Dick and Harry on the side," Vance explained bitterly.

"And is that what you think I'm doing?" Janene asked hurtfully.

"Maybe, I don't know. But I can certainly recognize a woman's response to my love-making and whether you will admit it or not you wanted me just as much as I wanted you a few minutes ago." A heavy silence fell between them. Janene had no response to his words for in her heart she knew what he said was true. She had held nothing back in her response and she knew it. "How old are you? he asked abruptly a short time later.

"Twenty-six. Why do you ask?"

"Just curious, I guess. Go to bed Janene. Goodnight."

"Vance, I," she began.

"Go to bed,' he interrupted rudely repeating his previous command then adding firmly. "Goodnight, Janene." He turned away from her and strode to the wet bar near the entrance. She watched him mix a stiff drink. She found herself wanting to go to him to assure him that all women weren't cheats. Instinctively, she knew that now was not the time. He had withdrawn from her into a world of torment built for and by himself.

"Goodnight, Vance," she whispered softly as she passed by him and left the room.

# Chapter 4

It was a long time before sleep came to Janene that night. She tossed and turned in the huge bed, her thoughts in turmoil. Hours later she heard Vance stumble up the stairs.

She sensed he was thoroughly drunk. She lay rigid as his footsteps halted outside the bedroom door. For a frightening second, she half expected him to enter the room. She heard him curse softly and listened as his footsteps moved away. Presently, a door slammed and Janene knew he had gone to his room. It was sometime later when Janene fell asleep.

She awakened midmorning. She showered and dressed unhurriedly despite the lateness of the hour. Quietly, she let herself out of the room into the hall. Vance's bedroom door remained closed. She suspected that he might still be sleeping it off. She entered the dining room, planning to fix her own breakfast and not bother Dora .

The house was strangely quiet. it gave her and eerie feeling of being totally alone. She pulled open the heavy drapes to expose the outdoors. The dense fog still clung to everything. Involuntarily, she shuddered, wondering if it would ever lift. She passed through the doorway Dora had entered to serve them breakfast the previous afternoon and found as she had expected the kitchen. It was entirely empty. 'How strange,' she thought. 'Where was Dora?' She was contemplating what to make for breakfast when Vance's footsteps echoed behind her.

"I thought I heard you come downstairs. I forgot to tell you that Dora is off on the weekends so we'll have to fend for ourselves." He gave her a wan smile. "Can you cook?"

"Yes" she replied quietly. "You don't look so good this morning."

"Thanks," he answered grimly, " I don't feel so hot either. I really tied one on."

"Yes, I know," she said. "Sit down and tell me where things are and I'll fix breakfast."

"You know," he inquired sharply giving her a penetrating doubtful look. The fleeting temptation to tease him as he had done with her the day before crossed her mind but she discarded the idea. He looked so glum and contrite.

"I heard you staggering upstairs very late."

"I'm sorry. I didn't mean to wake you. I didn't did I?" his voice trailed off uncertainly.

"You went rather noisily to your room," she hastily supplied and his facial expression relaxed. "What would you like for breakfast?" she asked without giving him a chance to speak.

"Just coffee," came the gloomy reply. He sat down heavily resting his head on his hands as he leaned upon the table. Janene found the coffee and percolator and in a few minutes had coffee brewing. She opened the huge upright freezer. Soon sausage, bacon, eggs and toast were being prepared. She poured Vance a mug of hot coffee setting it before him on the table. He had not moved. She could not resist the impulse to touch him and placed her hand gently upon his shoulder as she leaned to place the coffee mug beside him. He caught her hand in his, raising his head to look at her through red rimmed eyes.

She kissed him lightly as he turned toward her. A quick tug on her arm unbalanced her so she sat rather heavily in his lap. Immediately, his arms encircled her drawing her closer against him, his head buried against her breast. He raised his head slowly, deliberately and firmly claiming her soft, unresisting lips. Janene steeled herself to remain passive and unresponsive as his lips and tongue probed her mouth seeking, demanding a response. The kiss continued, her senses heightened, her resistance melted and she returned the ardent demands of those tender yet commanding lips.

Eventually, he released her and she twisted to her feet. She reached the stove just in time to keep the bacon from burning. Not a word passed between them. She took two plates from the cupboard and filled each. She located silverware and one of the laden plates she sat in front of Vance, who was now watching her. The other plate she set opposite him on the table for herself. After refilling his coffee mug she then sat down at the place she had prepared for herself. She drank some coffee and began to eat. Vance tackled his plate hungrily despite that fact he had requested nothing but coffee.

"Stay with me," he pleaded huskily, swallowing the last bite of toast.

"I am," she smiled.

"No, I mean always. Not just until the fog lifts but after that, too. Stay here with me."

"Vance, that's ridiculous, I can't do that."

"Why not?" "I have a job, a career, my own life to lead."

"I've plenty of money. Quit your job and stay with me."

"No, Vance. It is no good," she answered, continuing with her breakfast. She glanced at him from beneath lowered lashes. She was openly puzzled by his plea and wondered just what had prompted such a remark in the first place. He was staring thoughtfully at his plate, toying with the remains of his breakfast, a curious unreadable expression upon his face.

The rest of the meal was completed in silence. Janene grew more and more uncomfortable searching vainly for something casual and light to say. She had not answered Vance further and he had not pursued the subject. She was grateful for that fact even though she suspected that his current thoughts dwelt upon the matter. She had now accepted that fact that she was irresistibly attracted to him, that she warmed and responded to his touch, to his nearness.

She realized how easy it would be to throw caution to the wind and say yes to him. Just as she knew such an answer would eventually lead her into his bed. She flushed with embarrassment as she realized where her thoughts were taking her. She had no doubts that he would be a thoughtful, passionate lover. The expertise of his kisses and caresses had shown her that he was not lacking in experience. He would take a woman beyond the brink of physical desire into a world of delight and ecstasy.

It was the doubts concerning her own abilities that assailed her. During the last year or so she had considered having an affair. Until now she had met no one with whom she could consider such a prospect feasible. Now, she found herself curiously unwilling to go through with it at all. Somehow, she doubted she could walk away from an affair with Vance Reeves unscathed by the experience. 'Your inexperience is showing,' she chided herself silently.

If only the blasted fog would lift. Then she could reasonably leave here, resume her life and put her emotions back into perspective. She was aware suddenly that Vance was watching her. In confusion, she avoided his eyes and began clearing away the breakfast dishes. She stayed purposefully out of his reach, busily occupying herself with cleaning the kitchen. Although Vance neither moved nor spoke, she was acutely aware of his presence, instinctively knowing that he missed no movement she made. His silence bothered and puzzled Janene, but, for the life of her she could think of nothing casual to say that would break the ominous silence. She was disgusted by her own ineptness at rising above a sensory level.

Finally the area tidy once more, she dried her hands and turned to look at him. As she had expected, he was watching her, his eyes veiled and expressionless, his body relaxed lazily.

"More coffee?" she asked.

He nodded and she refilled both of their mugs. He had risen and reached around her to retrieve his own steaming cup from the counter. His arm brushed hers and the touch seared her skin like a burn. She withdrew slightly. He seemed not to notice, taking the mug in both hands, he left the room. Janene stood several seconds, staring blankly through the window at the mist outside. She sipped her coffee absently, her composure slowly returning. Now that Vance was no longer watching her every move, the tension drifted out of her. She drained her cup and left the vessel on the counter beside the still half full electric percolator.

She left the kitchen, passing through the empty dining room. The study door was open and she could see Vance sitting at his desk. She hesitated at the bottom of the stairs torn between the fact that she had promised to help him with his correspondence this morning and the fact that she didn't at this precise moment want to be near him.

Decidedly, she ascended the stairs. For the next half hour she tidied the bedroom which had been hers for the past two nights. Finding nothing left to do, and concluding that she could not remain in the room all day, Janene stepped into the hallway. The door of the room Vance occupied each night was ajar.

Without conscious thought, she stepped across to the door and pushed it open. The room was a mess. Clothing was strung haphazardly about. The bedclothes lay in a rumpled heap. Automatically, she began to pick up. She made the bed and put the room in order. She had seen a laundry chute in the hall so she gathered up the strewn clothing and deposited it in the laundry bin.

Satisfied that all was in order, she finally forced herself to go downstairs.

# Chapter 5

Vance was still bent over the desk absorbed in his work. She returned to the kitchen pouring herself a cup of coffee. She unplugged the percolator and carrying it with her crossed to the study. Quietly, she approached the desk, he looked up as she neared.

"I brought you some hot coffee," she volunteered refilling the now empty mug that sat on his desk. Afterwards, she sat the coffee pot on the wheeled cart near the entrance.

"Thanks," he said abstractedly, returning his attention back to his work. She wondered vaguely if she ought to leave but decided against doing so.

"Did you want me to do some typing now?" she asked hesitantly.

"If you like," he replied coolly then added. "It is not absolutely necessary if you would rather not."

"Oh, I don't mind really. It will give me something to do. Just tell me what you want typed and show me where things are and I'll get busy."

He indicated a small desk table which Janene had not noticed earlier. She went over to it and uncovered the electric typewriter. She found paper and other needs inside one of the drawers and put the machine in readiness. She, also, discovered a shorthand pad and several sharpened pencils.

"I have to dictate answers to these letters first."

His voice was impersonal and contained none of its usual warmth and friendliness. "Do you think you can manage or shall I write out my answers?"

"We'll never know until we try," she said her business-like tone taking its cue from his.

"Fine, then shall we begin?" without waiting for her reply he added, "Bring that chair nearer the desk." He arose and drew open the draperies revealing the mist covered garden below. He stood looking outside so long that Janene thought he had forgotten her when he suddenly began to dictate. Rapidly her pencil flew across the pad recording the words he spoke. He spoke slowly but steadily, his voice sharp and businesslike. He had dictated three letters before he finally paused asking,

"Am I going to fast for you?"

"I don't think so. I think I have it all," she answered crisply.

"Read it back to me then," he commanded. In a clear well-modulated voice she reread her scrawling script. When she had finished he nodded appreciatively. He had returned to his seat during her transcribing and sat with his long legs propped upon the desk corner.

"Fine. I'll dictate a couple more and that should do it." Almost at once he was on his feet dictating again. She recorded four more letters before he stopped. "That's all." he remarked reseating himself at the desk.

"Would you like me to read these back?" she asked in her most professional tone.

"That won't be necessary. You'll find addresses on these papers. Sign each "Sincerely yours," and I'll read and sign them all later." It was after two when Janene finished the last letter. She laid them neatly on his desk for his signature. At some time during the typing of the second letter, Vance had left the room without a word.

He had not yet returned. Janene rubbed her neck wearily, turning to view the outdoors. The fog continued to linger but it seemed not to be so heavy and tiredly she wondered if it might be lifting at last.

Her stomach growled and she realized sharply that she was hungry. It occurred to her that she had not taken a lunch break. Then she remembered that Dora wasn't about and if she wanted something to eat she had better fix it herself. She wondered absently where Vance had taken himself off to and thinking perhaps she ought to fix lunch for both of them.

As if on cue, he entered the front door scraping his feet noisily on the entry way mat. She waited self-consciously, hoping he would go on upstairs. Instead, he came into the study, his black hair waving messily from the dampness outside.

"Finished?" he asked.

She nodded her reply. "Have you had lunch?"

"No, I was just about to fix something," she announced moving to walk past him.

"Good, I'm starved. I'll help you." She would have much rather he'd stay behind in the study but she swallowed her comment. He followed her into the kitchen. "How does soup and sandwiches strike you?" he asked peering into the recesses of the refrigerator.

"Fine," she answered. She rinsed the percolator and prepared a fresh pot of coffee.

"Okay, I'll make the sandwiches, you make the soup." He handed her a bowl containing turkey broth and meat. Janene made a thickening and soon a rich aroma filled the room. Vance sliced thick slices of ham and cheese and competently made several sandwiches.

"Shall we eat in the den?" he asked lightly.

"Fine, maybe we can catch the weather report." Janene returned.

"Still hoping the fog will lift?" he quipped caustically.

"Well, I can't stay here forever," she answered sharply and instantly wished she could recall the remark.

"I don't know," he took up her comment as she had known he would. "I don't think I'd mind at all. In fact, I can think of several distinctive advantages." He winked rakishly. Janene bit her tongue, deciding to ignore the obvious taunt. She picked up the tray of sandwiches and soup, leading the way toward the den. Vance followed closely with a tray laden with cups, silverware and percolator.

As before, they sat on the couch, the coffee table serving as a receptacle for their food trays. It was a little after three and too early for a newscast. Vance located a mystery thriller. They ate in silence watching the movie.

Later as she cleared way the dishes, Janene found herself wondering if this was what living with Vance would be. Halfheartedly, she almost wished the fog would never lift so she might have the chance to find out. Her musing was cut short by Vance's entrance into the kitchen.

"Good news, Kitten," he said coming up behind her.

"Oh?"

"Yep, according to the forecast, there's a chance the fog will lift tomorrow. You can go home after all." She had turned toward him and he stood at arms length in front of her.

She nodded and starred past him, her feelings in a state of such confusion that she wanted to avoid his gaze at all costs.

"You don't seem gloriously happy'?" he commented drily. "I rather expected you'd dance a jig. You won't have to bear my company any longer." he added sarcastically.

Hesitantly, she turned and met his gaze. "There's nothing wrong with your company. I'm really grateful for everything."

"You could have fooled me?" he retorted sharply.

"Vance, I'm sorry I've disappointed you. Can't we just be friends?"

"I doubt it, Kitten. Friendship doesn't seem to be what I want from you," he added spinning about and heading toward the den. Unconsciously she reached out, her hand catching his forearm lightly. He halted as she said softly, her voice breaking throatily as she spoke.

"Won't I ever see you again?" His hand covered hers. He looked down at her questioningly.

"Do you want to?"

"Yes, I think I should like that very much."

"Why?"

"Does there have to be a specific reason?" she asked. His eyes locked with hers and he gazed intently into her eyes. It was as if he was trying to read something within the deep blue depths.

"No, I guess not," he said abruptly, pulling away from her light grasp. She followed him into the den. He began mixing them a cocktail. Janene sat down on the couch. Later, he brought her drink, handing it to her. Their fingers touched lightly as the glass changed hands. He withdrew quickly. He set his glass on the coffee table and for the next few minutes busied himself building and lighting a fire. It was dark now but they turned on no lights. He sat down beside her on the couch though he made no attempt to touch her. His manner, as it had been all day was coolly aloof. The fire blazed brightly.

Janene watched the glaring flames hypnotically. She was aware that Vance had lit a cigarette and was smoking, calmly relaxed on his end of the sofa. She stole a stealthy glance his direction. He was staring straight into the fire. In the dim light, she could see the furrowed, thoughtfulness of his brow. She resisted the sudden impulse to slide closer to him. Her fingers itched with the longing to entwine themselves in his dark wavy hair.

An overwhelming desire to feel his arms about her, to give herself over to the pleasure his lips could give her, engulfed her. Firmly, she pulled her eyes away from him to once more stare at the blazing flames, as they lapped hungrily at the pile of logs. How long they sat in silence, each lost in his or her own thoughts, Janene had no idea. She was brought to attention by Vance's low voice.

"We could get married." Janene turned to face him in startled bewilderment. She could not see his eyes but sensed that he was watching alertly for her reaction.

"Vance Reeves are you proposing to me?" she stammered nervously.

"Yes, I guess I am." his voice was so low she had difficulty hearing him.

"Why?" she asked softly.

"Hell, I don't know. I want you to stay with me." he replied gruffly. "I just thought it seemed like a good idea."

She said nothing partly because she didn't know exactly what to say and partly to give him time to explain, to tell her he loved her. He arose abruptly and flicked on the desk lamp. He picked up the letters she had typed earlier that afternoon and began reading through them quickly, affixing his signature to each. Puzzled, Janene watched him from her curled position on the couch.

"Well?" he asked moments later when his task had been completed.

"Well, what?" she countered vaguely.

"You haven't answered my question?"

"What question?" she implored stiffly.

"I'll be damned. You are really a cool one. A guy asks you to marry him and minutes later you've forgotten all about it."

"I didn't forget. I just didn't think you were serious," she explained.

"Well, I am. I'd like an answer. As for why I want to marry you, I'm tired of living alone. I'm tired of coming home to an empty house. The last two days have made me realize just what I've been missing. You are easy to be with. I meant it when I asked you earlier to stay with me. I think I know why you wouldn't agree. I've been going through my own private hell the last twenty four hours. I just can't let you go,"

He paused and walked around the desk to the window. There he stood, his back to her staring out into the night. Janene was unsure how to cope with this new situation. So far, he had not mentioned love and deep within her something stirred, telling her that she could never commit herself to marriage with a man who didn't love her. She admitted to herself that although she might not be hopelessly in love with this tall stranger, she was dangerously close. Still, she knew if he didn't love her it wouldn't be enough.

# Chapter 6

Suddenly, there was a sharp noise. Janene turned toward the fire expecting to see an exploding ember. Vance's loud cry of agony caused her to jump to her feet, her eyes flashing in his direction. She saw him slump forward and crumple to the floor. Someone screamed. Belatedly, she realized the scream came from her own throat. She rushed across the room.

"Stay down," he shouted hoarsely. She watched him crawl laboriously away from the window then collapse backwards as he hoisted himself into a sitting position against the end of the desk. She knelt beside him. "Close the drapes," he whispered weakly, "but stay to the side away from the window."

She did as he ordered without question. With the drapes drawn, she hurried back to him. "Vance, what's the matter?" she asked in a frightened, awed voice.

"I've been shot," he said taking his hand slowly away from his side. Blood covered his hand and sweater. She shoved a clenched fist against her mouth to stifle the scream she felt rising again in her dry throat.

"Darling, what can I do?" she asked softly. He smiled wanly. "Now, the lady calls me darling. You do choose your times, Kitten."

"Vance, we have to stop the bleeding and call a doctor and the police," she urged frantically.

"You take care of it, Kitten. I'm afraid I'm slightly

indisposed. The address book on the desk. Dr. Wyatt." he whispered. Janene was on her feet instantly. She called the doctor, explained the emergency quickly then dialed the police. The telephoning finished she knelt again beside Vance.

His face was ashen, his eyes closed. For a moment she thought he was dead. She buried her face against his shoulder crying helplessly. The eyelids flickered and opened as he tried to smile. His arm encircled her but he hadn't the strength to hold it there. "Take it easy, honey. I'm still among the living. You aren't rid of me yet."

"1 never want to be rid of you, silly." she whispered softly her heart in her eyes.

"Sure?" he asked meekly his eyes focused upon her face.

"Very, sure. Vance, shouldn't you be quiet. You are still bleeding badly." He tried to nod but his eyes closed as he slipped near unconsciousness.

The next ten minutes were the longest Janene had ever spent. She heard the police sirens drawing near, finally. Carefully, she eased herself from the dead weight of Vance's arm. "Where are you going?" he managed to murmur.

"Nowhere, darling," she whispered soothingly, kissing his forehead lightly. "I'm going to let the police and doctor in." She hurried to the front door, arriving just as the police car stopped outside. The two officers strode in through the open doorway followed by a bespectacled little man with a black bag. Vance was unconscious. The doctor knelt beside him quickly. He indicated that the officers should help move Vance into a completely supine position. Vance moaned as they eased him flat to the floor.

The officers began throwing questions at Janene, few of which she could answer. One of the officers discovered the bullet lodged in the top edge of the desk. It had apparently passed completely through the side of Vance's body. The ambulance attendants arrived. Vance's inert form was carried to the vehicle. Janene grabbed her purse, coat and flew out the door behind them insisting that she was accompanying Vance to the hospital. The ambulance trip into nearby Brea was accomplished in less than ten minutes. In the waiting room of the hospital, Janene waited nervously. It occurred to her that she knew very little about Vance Reeves. She wondered if there was some family to notify. She didn't even know how to get hold of Charles or Dora.

Some thirty minutes later the doctor came into the room. "Miss?"

"Dawson," she supplied quickly.

"Ah, yes, Miss Dawson. You're fiancée will be fine. He has lost considerable blood and is weak but is now awake and bellowing like a caged bull. I had wanted to keep him here tonight, but he insists on returning home. I know Vance usually lets Charles and Dora off for the weekends. He will, however, need someone with him for the next couple of days."

"I'll be with him," Janene said without hesitation.

"Good, I don't expect any complications. The bleeding has been stopped. He may have considerable pain though. There may, also, be a fever. See that he takes two of these tablets every four hours and that he spends at least two days in bed. Otherwise, he could open up the wound and cause further bleeding. I'll see him Monday afternoon, unless his condition changes. If that should happen call me at once. Now, I think it wise for you to go to him before he brings down the entire hospital."

Janene followed the doctor down the corridor to the emergency recovery room. Vance was lying on the white sheeted bed growling hostilely at the attending nurse.

He spotted Janene at once. "Will you get me out of this damn place, honey?" he asked glaring at the doctor.

"In due time, Vance," the doctor soothed calmly. "Miss Dawson, here, assures me she'll take care of you so I've agreed to let you go home. Against my better judgment I might add."

Vance raise his eyebrows questioningly, his glance straying back to Janene. Then nodded to his unspoken question. "However," continued the doctor, "I'm going to evoke some conditions. First, I want the two of you to return to Vance Manor in the ambulance. I want the attendants to see you safely into bed and I don't want you to get up for any reason until after I see you on Monday. Miss Dawson will attend to your needs. Is that understood?"

"Yes," Vance replied meekly.

"Fine," the doctor said quietly turning to Janene. "Is there a bed urinal at the Manor? He is not to risk getting up at all."

Janene shook her head. "I really don't know Dr.

Wyatt? You'll have to ask Vance." This the doctor did immediately.

Vance exploded with a violent oath. "You don't expect her to do that, too, do you, Wyatt? Good Lord, man, she isn't a nurse. "

"That's entirely up to you," the doctor replied coolly.

"I don't mind really, Vance," Janene hastily interjected.

"Well, dammit, I sure as hell mind."

"Fine," the doctor returned firmly. "Then you can just plan upon remaining here in the hospital until Monday afternoon." with that statement the doctor led Janene toward the door.

"I'll drive you back to Vance Manor, Miss Dawson, if you are ready?"

"Janene," Vance wailed sharply.

"Just a moment, doctor. I'll be right with you." She turned and went to Vance's bedside.

"You'd do that for me?" he whispered huskily an embarrassed flush coloring his still pale face. Janene nodded carefully hiding the amused smile that threatened to surface.

"All right, Wyatt, I don't like it but I'll play it your way since Janene doesn't object. Now, get me the Hell out of here." Vance ordered gruffly. Dr. Wyatt scowled thoughtfully but said nothing. In a few minutes the attendants appeared. They eased Vance on to the stretcher and carried him to the waiting ambulance. Vance grumbled continually on the trip back to Vance

Manor. In the darkness of the ambulance interior, Janene could barely contain her mirth at his prudish dishonor. It seemed incongruous with his earlier behavior, for he had certainly held no reservations regarding his ploy to entice her into his bed.

After fighting for two days to keep out of his bed she found his reluctance to have her tend his bodily needs more than laughable. She was glad he could not see her amusement for he was grumpy enough. The attendants carried him upstairs and deposited him at Janene's instruction in the room she had occupied the past few nights.

Vance was unable to argue about her decision because of the police officers who insisted upon interrogating him immediately regarding the shooting. This took nearly an hour and Janene could see Vance was totally exhausted. Finally, she determinedly escorted the officers downstairs insisting that Vance must rest and would answer no more questions until morning.

They informed her a police guard would be posted just outside the gate should there be any further disturbance or should she need anything. She was instructed to stay out of the den as most of police investigation would have to wait until daylight. Janene closed and locked the door behind the officers and went upstairs to Vance. His eyes were closed when she entered the room. Quietly she tiptoed to the edge of the bed and felt his forehead. He was slightly feverish. She started to leave when he spoke.

"Are you going to sleep with me?" he asked softly.

"I hadn't consider it," she responded lightly.

"I don't want you out of this room at night until this mess is cleared up or until I am able to get around."

"Don't be silly, Vance. There is a policeman outside. I'll leave both doors open and sleep directly across the hall. Then I can hear you if you need anything. I'll be just fine."

"No," he exclaimed harshly. "Either you stay in here with me so I know you are safe or I will get up here and now. This isn't some kind of game we are playing. Whoever did this shooting is deadly serious and until it's cleared up, I won't rest easy."

"That's black mail," she accused.

"You're right but I mean it. Besides your virtue is perfectly safe. I'm not exactly in condition to engage in a night of lusty frolic. Besides, this bed is wide enough for a whole damn army. Well," he said raising his shoulders in an effort to sit-up. She pushed him back gently.

"All right, Vance," she agreed quietly. "I'll sleep in here if you'll behave. I don't want you opening up that wound."

"I promise," he said soberly. "I can't do much else anyway." He chuckled throatily.

"What's so funny?" she snapped.

"I was just thinking. For the past three days, I've used every tactic at my disposal to maneuver you into sharing my bed and now when you finally agree, I can't take advantage of it."

"Idiot," she giggled. "If I thought you could, do you think I'd agree?"

"I might just fool you." he grinned.

"I seriously doubt it but I guess I'll have to take my chance. Anyway, I think one good punch in that side would change your mind."

Janene planted a light kiss full upon his lips then quickly retreated into the bathroom. She undressed, showered and put on her nightgown. When she returned to the bedroom, Vance was already asleep. She doused the light and slid beneath the sheets beside him. Exhaustion took over and she, too, fell immediately to sleep.

# Chapter 7

The next morning, Janene awakened to find Vance burning with fever. She gave him his medication and bathed his forehead with cool cloths. She could not get him to eat. Worriedly, she phoned Dr. Wyatt. He assured her that he had expected the fever and explained it was a normal part of the healing process particularly following a gunshot wound. He questioned her briefly, informed her that he did not see any immediate danger. In a vain effort to bolster her ego, he told her cheerily to carry on. All that day and the following night Vance's fever raged.

From time to time, his mind cleared slightly enabling him to recognize her. Many times she wished she knew how to locate Charles or Dora. She had searched the desk in the study for some address or phone number but could make no sense out of Vance's sketchy listings. Not knowing the surname of the couple posed a real problem as Vance tended only to write surnames and accompanying phone numbers.

During the day, she left Vance's bedside infrequently, fearful that in his fevered state he would attempt to get out of bed and further injure himself. Sunday morning the police completed their investigation of the grounds and the study. The police car and guard remained outside the front entrance but she had received no information regarding their progress in the case.

Janene did not sleep in the bed with Vance that

night but instead had pulled one of the heavy leather chairs into a position near the bed. It was in this that she dozed briefly while Vance moaned and tossed with fever. The mist had grown thinner but still covered the outside world with its dreary greyish blanket. The house was frighteningly empty. The study window had been boarded up covering the broken hole through which the hateful bullet had entered. Although the study door now stood open, it took all of Janene's courage to keep herself form scurrying by it in fright each time she passed the doorway.

She was expected at work in the downtown youth organization where she worked as a field director Monday morning. She had concluded the following afternoon that under no circumstances would she be able to leave Vance in his present condition. She fully expected Dora and Charles both to appear that morning and welcomed the idea of someone else occupying the house.

Cramped and chilled she awakened before six. She felt Vance's forehead and he stirred silently. The fever seemed to have lessened slightly, and he was sleeping deeply. She showered quickly and changed into fresh clothing. By seven o'clock she had made coffee and some toast. As she ate her solitary breakfast, she wondered vaguely what time she could expect Dora.

Fearful that Vance might awaken during her absence, she left without tidying the kitchen. She crept softly into the bedroom. Vance was still sleeping peacefully, so she immediately retreated again.

In the kitchen, she tidied up and poured herself

another mug of coffee. The startling jangle of the telephone made her jump. Hesitantly she looked about the kitchen for the phone as it shrilled a second time. Not wasting time to locate the kitchen phone, she ran swiftly through and into the study lifting the receiver of the desk phone upon its fifth ring.

"Hello," she said breathlessly.

There was a brief silence before a woman's voice asked crisply, "Who are you?"

Janene ignored the question, waiting.

"Hello," the voice snapped rudely. "Are you still there? I'd like to speak to Vance." A pause, then "please" was added almost as an after thought.

"I'm sorry," Janene answered coolly. "Mr. Reeves is unable to come to the phone now. May I take a message?"

"No, yes, all right" the female voice replied crisply.

"Tell him to call Mona as soon as possible. By the way, who are you?" the voice asked again pointedly.

Again, Janene ignored the question.

"I will give Mr. Reeves the message. Does he have the number?" she retorted, her voice still professionally cool.

"He most certainly does, and make sure he calls me immediately."

The line went sharply dead. Janene replaced the receiver with a bang. 'What a rude person!' she thought angrily. Then, chided herself. After all, the woman was obviously puzzled, and possibly had reason to be hostile.

She ran upstairs swiftly, hoping the telephone had not disturbed Vance. It hadn't. She stood looking at him tenderly for several seconds, then, for the third time that morning, descended the stairs.

She glanced into the kitchen to see if Dora had arrived yet. There was still no sign of the housekeeper. She drew open the draperies as she passed back through the dining room, noting that the mist had cleared, finally. Faint rays of California sunshine were beginning to lighten the horizon, and she suspected that, by noon, the last evidence of fog would be burned away.

A glance at her watch informed her it was nearly 8:30. In a few minutes she would have to call her office. She was nervous, tired, and worried. Rummaging around the top of the study desk, she finally located a partial pack of cigarettes. Although she rarely smoked, and practically never in the morning, she lit a cigarette with trembling fingers and inhaled deeply. Again she wished fervently that either Charles or Dora would arrive so she would not feel so completely alone.

She stole another glance outside. The police car, too, was gone. Evidently they had decided there was no further danger, and that they no longer needed to guard the house. Instead of comforting her, she became more uneasy than ever. It had helped somehow to know the guard was just outside. Now she was truly alone. The thought depressed her, and she began to cry softly.

After a few minutes, she pulled herself together and walked back to the desk. She lifted the receiver, dialed and waited.

Presently a warm friendly female voice answered.

"Orange County Council of Camp Fire Girls, may I help you?"

"Nancy, this is Janene."

"Oh, hi Janene. What can I do for you?"

"Listen Nancy, can you inform Mrs. Billings that I won't be in for a few days or is she there?"

"No, she isn't in yet. What's wrong?"

"There's been a family crisis and I can't leave just yet. Please tell her I'll call later in the week and let her know definitely when I can return to work."

"Okay. I hope it's nothing serious, Janene? Is there anything I can do?"

"It is rather, but nothing I can explain over the phone. No, there is nothing anyone can do, but I may not be able to get in to work at all this week. Please tell Mrs. Billings for me, and Nancy, if she wants to call me, give her this number." Quickly Janene read the number off the phone label. Janene replaced the receiver quickly and sat staring at the silent phone for several seconds.

Decidedly, she picked it up again and dialed. This time her wait was longer. Finally there was an answer.

"Mom," she paused, then continued. "I'm going to being staying here in Brea for a few days. I've taken another week off from work to help a friend. Should my boss call, cover for me. I told her it was a family crisis and I was needed at home." There was another lengthy pause, then Janene replied. "Nothing, Mom. I'll explain it all when I write. Don't worry please. I don't think Mrs. Billings will call you, but I couldn't fully explain over the phone, so I said the first thing that popped into my head.

Please, Mom no more questions. I have to go now." There was another pause. "No, Mom, I'm not in any trouble. Take care. Goodbye."

Janene hung up the phone with a determined bang, regretting slightly that she had called her family at all. She shook her head thoughtfully. She hated any kind of deceit, but at the moment there was no way she could explain. Had she told them about Vance, his being shot etc. they would never have understood. Furthermore, they would have been frantic with worry. No, it was better this way. Puzzled they might be, but they would trust her judgment and wait for an explanation. If there was a chance, she'd write them soon.

Janene went back to the kitchen refilled her coffee mug and walked upstairs, carrying it carefully with her. Vance was still asleep. She sat down in the heavy chair, then immediately arose again. She laid a fire from the kindling and logs stacked near the fireplace, and soon the chill of the room began to dissipate as the fire blazed warmly.

She retrieved her coffee mug, and sat down in the remaining chair facing the fire, sipping the hot liquid thoughtfully.

Her thoughts concluded that for some reason, neither Dora nor Charles were coming in today. Since she knew little or nothing of Vance's affairs, there was no alternative but to sit and wait. She'd be here if he needed anything, outside of that, there was nothing she could do. Arriving at this conclusion, she began to relax. She finished her coffee, sat the empty mug on the floor beside the chair, and curled up, her eyes on the blazing flames.

Janene was sleeping when she awakened to hear a hoarse voice yelling.

"Dammit, Dora, where are you?"

She jumped up, stumbling, and hastily ran to the bedside.

Vance's eyes were open, and with a groan of pain, he had fallen back against the pillows, having vainly tried to sit up.

His eyes blinked dazedly as he stared at her.

"What are you doing here?" he asked weakly. "Where's Dora? Oh, God, I hurt. What the hell's going on here?"

"Take it easy, Vance, you mustn't re-open the wound." Janene answered, gently placing a hand on his now cool forehead. "You're fever has broken. Good. Are you hungry?"

"I'm starved," he growled. "What the hell do you think you're doing?" he asked, irritably, as she straightened the bedclothes and proceeded to fluff up his pillow.

"I'm trying to fix your bed," she answered coolly.

"I can see that, but that's not what I mean, and you damn well know it. Now, where's Dora?"

Patiently, Janene looked down at him. "I've no idea where Dora is. I haven't seen her since Friday evening" she answered evenly. A foul curse escaped his lips as he again tried to move. The pain paled his face, and he lay back, his eyes closed, his mouth tightened in a thin grimace.

"Vance, please be still. You are not to move until after Dr. Wyatt re-examines the wound this afternoon. Don't you remember being shot?"

His eyes flew open uncomprehendingly. He stared at her, then slowly she saw the memory flooding back, mirrored in his eyes as he recalled the incident.

Sensing that he needed time to get things straightened out in his mind, she said, turning away from the bed, "I'll go fix you something to eat. Just be still, and I'll be back shortly." With that, she disappeared.

Some twenty minutes later, she reappeared, bearing a tray laden with orange juice, coffee, two softly coddled eggs, and some toast.

Amid much groaning and ill-tempered protests, she eased pillows behind his back, and burying his head against her breast, eased him into a half-sitting position. When she tried to pull away from him, she realized his arms encircled her tightly. Carefully, not to hit his wounded side, she slid into a crouched position beside the bed, her head cradled against his chest. She looked up at him. His eyes were warm and tender. She raised her head to meet the onslaught of his lips. When he released her, she moved deftly from his arms, and placed the tray carefully across his lap.

"Do you want me to help you?" she asked kindly.

"I can manage, I guess." She left him then, and sat down in the chair at the foot of the bed. She watched him eat silently. When he had completely devoured everything, she removed the tray. She poured him some more coffee, and lit a cigarette, which she handed to him, placing an ashtray within easy reach. He had not spoken, but his eyes followed her every move admiringly.

She retrieved her own coffee mug, poured some of the liquid for herself, and curled in the chair, as she awaited the questions she sensed were coming.

"What day is it?" he asked.

"Monday."

"What happened to Sunday?"

"You were raging with fever all day Sunday, and until you awakened awhile ago."

"I see," he mused. "Aren't you supposed to be at work?"

"I called in. They aren't expecting me for a few more days."

"And you've been here, ever since the shooting, alone?"

She nodded. "Until this morning, a police car and guard were stationed outside. I don't know where Dora and Charles are, and since I didn't know their last names, I was unable to call them. You refused to stay at the hospital, so I agreed to take care of you."

"That was damn inconsiderate of me," he sputtered.

"I didn't mind really."

"Have you stayed in here with me all the time?" he asked, wonderingly. She nodded her head, allowing him to draw his own conclusions. His eyes strayed to the other side of the bed, and back to her. Even though she had straightened the bed, it was fairly obvious that someone had slept there recently, and since he could move only slightly, she knew what thoughts crossed his mind. She chose not to comment further.

"So, I got you to stay with me after all," he murmured huskily. "I don't think I planned to go to such extremes though." He was thoughtfully silent for awhile. Laboriously, he eased himself to a flatter position on the bed.

"Take a couple of these damn pillows away, will you?" he asked gruffly. She did as he asked, noting his tight-lipped grimace as he fell backwards. She disappeared into the bathroom, returning with a glass of water, and two tablets.

"What's that?" he asked, irritably.

"Some medicine."

"I don't want it."

"Vance," she snapped. Their eyes met. Hers did not waver, and finally he nodded. Putting her hand behind his head, she lifted it gently, raising the glass to his lips as he plopped the pills into his mouth. When he had swallowed them, she arose and returned the glass to the bathroom. She re-seated herself in the chair. He had relaxed, and she had about decided he had fallen asleep again when he spoke.

"I'd forgotten, but I had planned to leave for New York, this morning, so I gave Dora and Charles two weeks off."

"Why were you going to New York?"

"I needed to get away from everything for awhile, so I was going to take a short trip. Then, after I met you, and you came back here with me, I forgot all about it.

The fog settled in, and I decided to talk you into spending some time with me instead. I liked having you around, and I rather thought we might have some fun together. I soon realized my plan would take a little doing, as you weren't exactly keen on the idea of staying with me. That kind of puzzled me, since most women nowadays jump at the chance for a good time, especially if the guy isn't strapped for money."

"I see, and you thought I'd drop everything, and go along for the ride," Janene added, caustically.

"That's about it," he agreed.

"I'm sorry I disappointed you," she said, picking up the tray, and walking toward the door.

"Where are you going?" he asked, sharply.

"I thought I'd clear away this mess, and make some more coffee," she answered coolly.

"Forget it, and stay here with me."

"I don't think so."

"Why, have I made you angry?"

No, I just need to stretch my legs a bit."

"Okay, but don't stay away too long."

She didn't answer that. Instead, she walked down the stairs, her eyes filling with tears. 'Well, Janene,' she scolded, as she descended the stairs. 'What did you expect anyway? You should have known his proposal Saturday night was merely a ruse to weaken your defenses. Hadn't he practically said as much just now? So you've fallen in love with him. You aren't the first woman to fall in love with the wrong man, and I'm sure you won't be the last.'

# Chapter 8

Blinking her eyes dry, she cleared away the mess created preparing Vance's breakfast, and re-tidied the kitchen. She made another percolator of coffee, her thoughts churning erratically. First and foremost, she had to keep her real feelings hidden from Vance. If she was to be successful in that endeavor, she needed to figure out a way to get away from here as soon as possible. There was no hope of depending on either Charles or Dora to be around to tend him, and regardless of her own feelings, she couldn't leave him alone. Panic settled in. What could she do? There had to be something. Suddenly, it came to her. Dr. Wyatt was due in a few hours. She would tell him she'd lose her job unless she returned to work immediately. She'd enlist his aid in securing a practical nurse to stay with Vance until he recovered. After all, he could afford one. She'd then pack, call a taxi, and be home before nightfall. Having decided on a course of action, she felt better. She hesitated facing Vance immediately, so rather than do so, poured herself more coffee, lit a cigarette, and sat down glumly at the kitchen table. She was lost in thought when the door chime caused her to jump hastily to her feet. Butting her cigarette, she sped to the front door. Rather belatedly, she remembered to ask who it was before opening the door.

"Dr. Wyatt," came the curt answer.

Janene opened the door eagerly, greeting the doctor with a warm smile.

"How's our patient?" he asked.

"The fever has broken. He's pesty and - "

At that moment, an irate voice called, "Janene, who's at the door? Dammit, answer me."

"Need I say more?" Janene winked at the doctor as she called serenely upstairs, "It's Dr. Wyatt, Vance. He'll be up in a moment. Keep your cool."

They heard Vance grunt irritably, and the doctor smiled knowingly at Janene. "Not the world's most agreeable patient, eh?"

"That's an understatement," she replied. "Before you go up, doctor, could I speak to you privately for a few minutes?" she asked, hesitantly.

She led him into the study, and quietly closed the door.

"I've learned that Charles and Dora are on a two week vacation, as Vance had planned to take one himself these next two weeks. I can't stay here indefinitely. I will lose my job if I don't get back to work by tomorrow or the next day. I was wondering if you could arrange for a private nurse to attend Mr. Reeves while he's recuperating?"

"I'm sure that will be no problem, but I was under the impression you were engaged to Vance. Doesn't he know you're leaving?"

"No, I haven't told him yet. We are just friends. I didn't correct the officer's impression the other night simply because at the time, it didn't seem important," Janene lied.

The doctor nodded vaguely. "All right, I'll see what I can do, now I'd better get up to Vance before he climbs out of that bed in sheer stubbornness."

Janene did not follow the doctor out of the room, but instead paced nervously about as she waited.

It was better than thirty minutes before the doctor descended the stairs again.

"How is he?" she asked genuinely concerned.

"On the mend. He should stay in bed a couple more days, but he can begin to move around a bit, as long as he doesn't overdo it. The wound is healing nicely. I changed the dressing, and I don't think there's much chance of him re-opening it, if he behaves himself. He'll be so sore for another 48 hours and that the pain itself will keep him in line."

"I'm glad," she said.

"I'll check on a nurse, and get back to you later this afternoon. You'd better try to get some rest yourself. You look worn out."

"I am a little tired, but I'll be fine. Thank you."

She let the doctor out the door, and was silently relieved. She had secured the lock, and was leaning easily against the door, when Vance called sharply, "Janene." She didn't answer. "Janene," he called again, "please come up here."

"All right," she answered. Steeling herself to passiveness, she slowly ascended the stairs, and entered the bedroom.

"Yes, what do you want, Vance?" she asked lightly.

"I want to talk to you," he snapped. "Sit down."

She started to comply by sitting in the chair, when he commanded sharply, "Not there, here beside me where I can see you."

She hesitated briefly, then crossed to the bedside. He caught her wrist as she came within reach, and pulled her to sit beside him.

"What's this I hear about you leaving?" he asked crossly. "Can't take it after all, right?"

She ignored the sarcasm, and avoided his eyes. "I have to get back to work, Vance, or I'll lose my job."

"I thought you said they wouldn't be expecting you for another few days," he stated deliberately.

"I did, but my boss called later, and said that if I was not in the office by Wednesday morning, she'd have to find a replacement. I asked Dr. Wyatt if he could arrange for a private nurse, since neither Dora nor Charles are around. Oh, by the way, someone called Mona phoned earlier, too. She wanted you to call her immediately. I'm sorry, but I forgot to relay the message until just now."

She looked at him casually, silently complimenting herself on her quick thinking. She had sensed he was about to accuse her of lying, not having heard the phone ring since she'd left his room. She could see the confusion in his eyes as he realized he must have heard neither call.

"When are you leaving?" he asked softly.

"As soon as the nurse can be obtained."

"Would it change anything if I asked you to stay?" She shook her head, and arose. She walked to the window, and stared down into the glistening wet garden below, now bathed in warm sunshine.

"I can't figure you out," he mused presently. "You could have gotten a nurse Saturday night, instead of staying here yourself, while I ranted and raged in fever."

"Yes, I could have," she agreed in a low voice. "I just didn't happen to think of it. Besides, I expected Dora and Charles to report as usual this morning."

"I see," he said. A heavy silence fell upon the room. Janene wanted to escape, but could think of no graceful exit, so she remained at the window.

"Are you sure it's your job that brought about your sudden decision to leave?"

Janene tensed, and was relieved to find her voice calm as she answered:

"Of course, what else can it be?"

"I wonder," he muttered more to himself than her. She turned away from the window. From his propped position in bed, he was staring straight ahead, his brow furrowed in concentration.

"I think I'll go fix something to eat." She wasn't particularly hungry, but it was the only excuse she could think of to get out of the room, and away from his nearness. "Would you like anything?"

He nodded absently.

"What sounds good?" she asked solicitously.

"What, oh, soup is fine," he answered vaguely.

Later, standing before the open refrigerator door, Janene debated upon a menu. Finally deciding on potato soup, she busily tackled the task. Nearly an hour later, she climbed the stairs with a tray laden with bowls of steaming potato soup, crackers, and hot buttered rolls. For dessert, she had prepared a soft custard pudding.

As she entered the bedroom, Vance greeted her with a boyish smile that was nearly her undoing. "It sure smells good," he commented, sniffing deeply. "Are you going to eat with me?" She nodded as she placed the tray on the dresser, and moved to aid him into a sitting position.

She saw him lift himself bodily, and slide forward, his shoulder muscles rippling. Hurriedly, she secured two pillows behind him. Beads of perspiration formed on his forehead depicting the effort the move cost him. Her eyes softened sympathetically.

"Janene, I want…." His voice faltered and petered out, as the look she cast him was one of remote coolness.

She arranged the tray across his lap after removing her own portion from it. Gently, she tucked a napkin into his pajama top collar. Her fingers tingled as they contacted the warm flesh of this upper chest. She avoided his eyes, acutely aware that his were intently fixed on her face.

She took her own meal to the nearby chair. As she sat down, he said, "This is good. Did you make all this from scratch?"

She smiled pleased. "Yes, I told you I could cook."

"You sure can," he smacked appreciatively.

He had completely finished his meal before she was half through. "Do you want something else?" she asked.

"No, finish your lunch. I'll wait," he answered.

She was unable to eat everything as he had, and presently she arose and removed his tray. She was stacking things up to take downstairs when he asked, "Would you light me a cigarette, and is there any coffee?" She lit the cigarette, and handed it to him. Then, she picked up the tray and descended to the kitchen.

She poured two mugs of coffee, and put them, and the percolator, on a tray, and returned to the bedroom.

She drank her coffee, restlessly pacing about the room. She added wood to the fire, but could not remain in one place.

"Are you so anxious to be out of my company?" he asked softly, after several minutes had elapsed.

"Of course not," she snapped crossly. "Why do you ask?"

"No particular reason, you just seem ill at ease and restless. You're like a caged cat."

"I'm sorry," she murmured and sat down in the chair near his bed. "I guess I'm a little restless at that. I'm not used to being idle that's all."

"You look tired. Did you sleep at all last night? Damn little, I bet," he growled. "Why don't you stretch out here on the other side of the bed and rest. If I hear the phone or doorbell, or want anything, I'll awaken you, okay?"

As she hesitated, he retorted peevishly, "Look, I won't touch you, and you need the rest. Come on."

Reluctantly, she rounded the bed and stretched out wearily. He was right, she thought, I am tired. She was so tired that even his nearness seemed not to affect her, and in a few moments, she was sound asleep.

The room was in total darkness when she

awakened. For a brief instant, she could not remember where she was. Heavy labored breathing made her body draw rigid as she realized she was not alone. Suddenly conscious memory returned, and she turned in the bed.

# Chapter 9

"God damn," came the muttered curse.

"Vance, what is it, what's the matter?" Complete silence. She inched quickly forward on her stomach to touch his arm tossing back the coverlet he had somehow managed to throw over her as she had slept.

"I'm sorry," he spoke softly in the darkness, as her hand found the warm muscled flesh of his upper arm. "I didn't mean to wake you."

"That's all right. Just a moment, I'll turn on a light." She bounded off the bed quickly, and was about to switch on the light when his sharp "No" halted her.

"Why ever not?" she asked stunned. "One can't see a thing in here."

"Good," he said, the bed creaking, as he grunted and groaned.

"Vance, what's the matter with you?" she could just distinguish his bulky torso in the faint light from the bathroom door, and realized he was trying to get out of bed. Forgetting the light, she hastily rounded the bed to his side.

"What do you think you're doing?" she asked angrily.

"If you must know, I'm trying to get to the bathroom. I have to take a leak," he added crudely.

"Well, for God's sake, why didn't you say so? I'll help you. Just let me turn on the light here, and then you can at least see what you're doing," she crossed in front of him, fumbling to find the night stand and, in turn, the light switch. His arm shot out blocking her movement.

"Don't turn on the damn light," he rasped.

"Vance, why?"

"Just do as I ask," he said.

"But you can't go stumbling thought the room in the dark. You might open your wound."

"God, Janene," he muttered hoarsely, "don't you realize I haven't any pants on, and I don't think this damn pajama top is long enough to hide me adequately. I don't relish parading around in this state of dress, or undress, in front of anyone. Do you understand?"

Despite herself, Janene could not help bursting into laughter.

"What do you find so damn funny?" he roared hotly.

"You," she giggled. "I don't care if you're stark naked. Either I help you, turn on the light, or you crawl right back in bed and I'll bring you the bed pan."

"Like hell you will, you'll do nothing but go around to your side of the bed and let me alone," he snapped. As the impact of what she said hit him, he hesitated. "What do you mean, bring me a bed pan? Have you done that before?"

"I have, and what's more, who do you think put that pajama top on you in the first place?" she retorted with obvious annoyance. "I assure you, you didn't come from the hospital in that state of dress or undress," she giggled, using his own words.

"I didn't realize," he murmured contritely.

"Well, now you do. Which is it to be?"

"Leave the light off, and come over here and help me," he capitulated, none too gracefully.

She moved to his left side, and sat down beside him on the bed.

He put his arm heavily around her shoulders as he used his right arm as a brace, and she rose, hoisting him with her. He swayed weakly, but she held his hand on her shoulder tightly, her other hand steadying his back. She could not reach around his waist for fear of hitting the wounded area of his right side. He drew a deep, painful breath and they started moving slowly toward the bathroom door. Grabbing the doorway, he released her from his hold, using the door frame for balance. "Thanks," he murmured. "I can manage from here." As she hesitated, he added crudely, "What do you want to do, hold it for me?" came the cruel stinging sneer.

Blushing, she left him. As she found her way across the room to the fireplace, her anger blazed furiously. Why is he so damn crude and ornery? She thought hatefully. She'd be damned if she'd help him again unless he asked nicely. Why should she care if he split his damn side open? She did care though, and reluctantly, she admitted that until she left here, she'd have to take whatever obscenities and anger he chose to vent upon her.

She busily re-kindled the fire, her anger subsiding. She knew instinctively that his irritable sarcasm was not directed against her personally, but rather toward his inability to cope with his condition on his own. He was a strong, virile, active man, and his dependency could not be an easy thing for him to bear.

She heard the toilet flush, and a muttered oath and groan, but she did not turn nor rush to him. She tensed as she listened to his shuffling movements, and heaved a relieved sigh as she heard the bed creak, protesting as he lowered his heavy frame upon it.

Still, she stood, arms folded, before the blazing firelight.

"Janene," he called softly. "Come here."

She made her way cautiously across the dark room to his bedside. She stood there quietly.

"Turn on the light, please?" he asked. She did so with relatively little fumbling for the switch. His hand caught her wrist as the lamp light flooded the room. She looked down at him, aware of the gentle concern and tenderness mirrored in her eyes. His face was ashen, beads of perspiration drenched his pale face.

"I'm sorry," he said softly. "I've no right to take my foul humor out on you. It's just such a damn inconvenience. Forgive me."

She nodded, "I know, and yes, I forgive you." She took the still-damp rag she had used earlier, to bathe his fevered face, from the night stand, and gently wiped the sweat from his face.

He clasped her hand in both of his, turning a palm against his lips. It took all her will to keep from jerking her hand away from his gentle caress, which created an aching longing to be in his arms.

"Did it hurt so much, darling?" she said softly, unaware that she'd used the endearment naturally.

He heard it though, and his eyes alerted instantly. Roughly, he grabbed her neck, his hand tangling in her hair, as he pulled her head back to gaze deeply into her eyes.

"Not half as much as another ache I have," he murmured softly, pulled her head down so their lips met. His kiss was punishingly brutal, the pressure bruising her mouth unmercifully. She tried to pull away, but his lips probed demandingly until he evoked the response he wanted. Only then did he release her mouth, as his lips traced a trail of fire along her cheek and temples, her neck, and finally claimed her lips again.

When he finally stopped kissing her, their breathing was heavy with unsatisfied desire. He cradled her head against his chest. She could feel his heart pounding, as she knew her own was doing. She rested, struggling for composure, his hot breath fanning the top of her head.

"Janene, why are you really leaving me?"

"I told you," she said quickly.

"I know what the hell you said, but I don't believe it. Not when you kiss me like that."

She raised up carefully. He did not try to hold her, but watched her intently.

"As I told you before, your expertise in that department is very difficult to combat."

"To hell with my expertise. You'd respond if I'd

never kissed a woman before in my life. I know you want me as much as I want you, no matter what you say to the contrary."

"Perhaps," she said non-committally.

"Janene, what are you trying to do to me? Surely you know how I feel about you. Why do you persist in running away from me?"

"Is that what I'm doing" she asked.

"You know damn well it is," he snapped back. "Go around to your side of the bed, and crawl up beside me. I want to hold you in my arms while we talk this thing out."

"I don't think that's such a good idea," Janene reflected, clearly aware of her own emotional state.

"Well, I do. If you don't, I'll lunge out of this bed, wound or not," he threatened, still lightly grasping one of her wrists.

"All right, Vance. If that's what you want," she agreed wearily.

She lay down on the bed beside him, her head cradled on his shoulder, his arm holding her lightly.

"Kiss me," he demanded. She turned her head slightly. His right hand tilted her chin, his head bending to claim her lips gently, tenderly, searchingly. This kiss was far more devastating to her senses than his previous brutal onslaught had been. Automatically, she edged closer, molding her pliant body against his. He turned to his side, ignoring any discomfort, and drew her even closer. Her arms entwined about his neck. She could hold back nothing.

"God, but I love you," he whispered hoarsely. "Stay here with me. Marry me." She did not answer.

"My darling kitten, I love you so much. Can't you love me a little?" he continued, his voice husky with emotion.

She gazed at him, and the love shining in her eyes must have satisfied him, for his lips claimed hers possessively.

"What about Mona?" she asked minutes later.

"Mona who?" he teased. "What does she matter? I love you. It's you I want for my wife."

"But you don't really know me," Janene protested, logically.

"What's to know? You can cook, you're kind and gentle, and besides that, you feel and taste good," he grinned, kissing her lightly.

"Well, I don't know anything about you," she added.

"Don't you want to marry me?" he asked impatiently. "Somehow I seem to remember you'd already said yes. Are you having second thoughts?" She hesitated, not answering.

He tilted her chin so their eyes met.

"Do you love me?" he asked soberly.

"Oh, darling Vance. Yes, I love you," she said happily, meeting his lips eagerly.

"I'm glad that's finally settled," he said, teasingly. "Now, when?"

"Anytime you want," she answered quickly.

"Well, I'd say right away, but I'm afraid I'm not

quite fit for a wedding night. But just as soon as this damn thing is healed, we'll fly to Las Vegas and get married. Right?" he paused, thoughtfully. "You don't want one of those big, fancy affairs, do you?" he asked intently.

"What if I said 'yes'?"

"Then I guess I'll have to suffer through it," he replied, meekly.

"Las Vegas is fine."

"Good! Now, one other thing, then you can hop to and fix me a steak. I'm ravenous," he commanded.

"And what's that?" she asked curiously.

"Are you still bent on leaving me tomorrow?"

"Do you want me to?" she asked.

"You know the answer to that without asking," he murmured softly against her hair.

"All right, I'll stay," she said. "I guess it doesn't really matter about my job now anyway."

"That's good, because I told Dr. Wyatt, when he called earlier, that you'd changed your mind."

"Why, you arrogant cad. You were pretty sure of yourself, weren't you?" she accused with rancor.

"Not really. I'd just decided what I wanted, and I was willing to try anything."

"You're disgusting, you know that, don't you?" she teased.

"Yep, so I've been told," he drawled lazily. Then, her gave her a hefty shove. "Scoot, woman. I'm hungry."

# Chapter 10

Janene was busy in the kitchen, fixing steaks and salad, when the doorbell rang. Cautiously, she inquired who it was.

"Detective Roberts. LAPD," the brusque voice answered.

Janene opened the door cautiously. The detective flashed his badge, and pushed the door open to enter.

"I'd like to see Vance Reeves. Who are you?"

Janene disliked the man's manner, finding it difficult to be civil.

"My name's Janene Dawson. Mr. Reeves is upstairs in bed. First door on the left," she added, as the detective mounted the steps.

"What's your position here?" the man asked rudely.

"I'm chief cook and bottle washer," Janene flung sarcastically, as she flounced toward the kitchen.

She could hear the man's hearty chuckle as he continued up the stairs.

Angrily, she cut up the fresh vegetables for a salad, and put some potatoes in the oven to bake. She was curious about the detective's visit, but she hesitated to join them in Vance's room. With everything but the steaks prepared for their dinner, she waited nervously for the detective to depart. It was over an hour longer before she heard the front door close, signaling the detective's departure.

Quickly, she broiled the steaks, expecting to hear

Vance calling for her at any time. The steaks broiled to delicate rarity, she competently fixed two plates on the tray, maneuvering to fit in two salad bowls and steaming coffee mugs. There was no way to carry the percolator, so she decided if they wanted more coffee later, she'd have to come back for it. She covered her salad with Roquefort dressing, debating on what Vance's taste might prefer. She finally decided on Thousand Island. Checking to see the stove was turned off, she picked up the tray, and started up the stairs, wondering if Vance would tell her about the detective's lengthy visit.

He was sitting up, leaning against the headboard, smoking. His brow furrowed worriedly as she entered. He smiled warmly as she approached the bed, but she noticed the smile did not touch his eyes. For the first time since she'd met him, they were hard and unexpressive. She arranged the tray on his lap for him, using the foot rest of the leather chair for her own table.

The telephone shrilled loudly before she had fully settled herself. Startled, she looked about questioningly. She had not previously noted a telephone in the room.

"It's on the other night stand, toward the back," he answered her unspoken question.

She scurried around the bed and picked up the offending instrument.

"Hello," she answered quietly.

"Oh, it's you again," came the caustic voice. "I'd like to talk to Vance." Placing her hand on the mouthpiece, she mouthed "Mona." He nodded, indicating he'd take it.

She picked up the phone, pulled the cord to allow some freedom, and sat it on the bed, handing him the receiver.

"Yes," was his crisp answer. She indicated the door, signaling she would leave him if he wished. He shook his head.

"Oh, that was just my nurse," he answered coolly.

Absently, Janene wondered why he hadn't said 'fiancee', but chided herself inwardly, realizing he probably didn't want to offer any explanations.

"Just a slight accident that's laid me up for a few days." A pause. "Oh, no, Mona, thank you, that won't be necessary. I'm being well-looked after." Another brief pause. "Fine, I will." He hung up the phone abstractedly, and went to work on his steak.

"This is first rate," he complimented, smiling. "You're some cook, did you know that? You've got dear old Dora beat all to hell."

Janene murmured her thanks, and they finished the meal in silence.

"Janene, bring some more coffee and come back shortly. I have to talk to you," he said, as she prepared to carry the remains of their meal downstairs.

"All right, but I'll wash up these things first. I'll hurry though."

"No, take your time. I can wait," he offered.

Janene was faintly puzzled by the coolness of his tone. Both his voice and eyes held a remote aloofness that she had not witnessed earlier.

Several minutes later, the kitchen tidy once again, she mounted the stairs with the hot percolator. He was sitting as she had left him. She noticed that he had pulled the phone nearer, so evidently, he'd been doing some telephoning. She poured fresh coffee in both mugs, and stoked the fire.

Vance had not spoken at all. She settled herself in the chair, tucked her feet beneath her, sipping at her coffee, waiting.

He lit a cigarette, cursing under his breath as the first one slipped from his fingers to the floor. She couldn't help but notice that he seemed nervous and disturbed.

"We're going to have to postpone our plans, kitten," he said, bluntly. Then, before she could comment, continued rapidly. "I've call Dr. Wyatt, and he's sending a nurse out tomorrow morning, early. I've decided it's best you leave, return to your job, and I'll be in touch later. There seems to be more to this shooting incident than I realized at first. I'm going to be tied up for a few weeks until this thing is cleared up. Under the circumstances, I feel it's best for you not to be left around here on your own. It will be easier if you are working. As soon as I'm able to get around, I'll have to leave for awhile. I've arranged to have the house closed up, and I've given Charles and Dora an extended leave of absence indefinitely. I want you to pack your things and be ready to leave first thing in the morning." He paused, both for breath, and to butt out the cigarette that was threatening to burn his fingers.

"I don't understand, Vance. Why can't I just go with you? Surely we could be married somewhere in route, unless you've decided you want out after all. Even if I can't go with you, why must I leave before you're completely recovered?"

"I know you don't understand," he said, his tone softer. "I can't explain. Just trust me."

"All right, Vance, if that's the way you want it. I won't pretend I'm not confused and anxious, but I can see you've made up my mind for me. Are you in any danger?"

"No," he replied quickly, but intuition told her he was lying. She waited for him to add some assurance or further explanation, but he didn't. Slowly, she stood up and walked to the bathroom. She gathered up her things, and re-packed her suitcase, leaving out only her nightgown. She carried the items out with her, depositing the suitcase on the floor near the bedroom door, and tossing the nightgown over the back of the chair.

She straightened Vance's bed, pushed the chair back to its place before the fire, and arranged the telephone and cord so it would be on the night table nearest him. Her movements were precise, and definite. She was acutely aware that his eyes watched her, but he said nothing. A curious feeling of foreboding settled over her. She tried vainly to shake it off. She knew she was hoping he'd call her into his arms, kiss away her doubts, and assure her that he'd only been teasing. However, deep inside, she knew he wouldn't. He hadn't explained the visit from the detective; he'd given her no reasons at all for his sudden change of mind. In no way could she make sense out of things. Before the detective's arrival, he'd been so keen upon her staying, so tender and loving, openly declaring his love for her, and now he was sending her away. Why? What had she done?

The room in order, she crossed to his bedside, gazing down at him steadily, uncaring that her heart was showing in her eyes. He met her gaze briefly, his eyes veiled and remote, giving her no clue whatsoever regarding his thoughts or feelings.

"Is there anything you want before I go to bed?" she asked hesitantly.'

"No, nothing," he answered coolly. "Aren't you sleeping here?"

"No, I'll use the spare room tonight. That's all right, isn't it?" giving him an opening if he chose to take it.

For a brief instant, as his eyes met hers, her heart stopped, but the fleeting glimpse of emotional depth was gone so quickly, she later believed she'd imagined it.

"I'm sure that's best. You need a good night's sleep."

She turned then, not wanting him to see the pain in her eyes. She grabbed her nightgown, and picked up her suitcase, leaving his door open.

"Goodnight, kitten," he called softly, as she crossed the hall. Even then, had he called her back, she would have swallowed her pride and ran into his arms. But he didn't. Quietly, she closed the door of her room. She undressed without haste, then slid between the sheets, turning off the night lamp. The faint lingering smell of his cologne and shaving cream emitted by the pillow tantalized her nostrils. She buried her head deep into its soft depths as the tears slid down her cheeks. Blessedly, the sleep of the exhausted was not long in coming.

It was early when she awoke. The sun rays on the eastern horizon brightened the room, for she had forgotten to draw the drapes the night before.

She sat up quickly, her mind confused by the unfamiliar surroundings. As recognition and remembrance flooded upon her, she thought worriedly of Vance. Then, painfully, the memory of their last conversation poured through her. Slowly, she got out of bed, and padded barefooted to the adjoining bathroom. A thorough facial splashing with cold water made her feel better. She dressed rapidly, brushed her hair, and teeth, applied a light lipstick, and closed up her suitcase with all her belongings except her handbag. After making the bed, she emerged quietly into the hall. She stole a look into Vance's room. He was half lying, half sitting in bed, his eyes closed. The ashtray beside his bed overflowed. His face was drawn and etched with tiredness. She wondered if he'd been in so much pain he hadn't slept.

She slipped out of her shoes and tip-toed cautiously into the room. She stared down at him, wanting to kiss away the lines that etched the corners of his mouth and eyes. She quietly removed the ashtray and emptied its contents in the fireplace.

She was replacing it on the night stand when he spoke.

"You don't have to be so quiet. I'm not asleep."

"Is it hurting?" she asked.

"No, just haven't been able to sleep. In fact, it doesn't seem near as sore today. I was up a couple of times already," he answered wearily. "How are you this morning?"

"Fine," she lied cheerfully. "Would you like some breakfast?"

"You needn't bother."

"It's no bother, do you want something or not?" she snapped waspishly.

"A little grumpy this morning, are we?" he grinned. "Okay, kitten, I'll have breakfast."

Janene's heart did a flip-flop at the warmth in his tone, but when she sought his eyes, he averted them quickly. She left the room, slipped into her shoes and hurried down stairs. She fixed breakfast quickly, and returned to the bedroom in a few minutes with a tray.

"Are you going to eat with me?" he asked, seeing only the serving for one on the tray. She shook her head as she arranged the tray across his lap. She could see that he'd been up again, and washed, for his hair was slightly damp. He had been sitting up when she had entered.

"Why?" he asked.

"I didn't think you wanted me to," she replied.

"Don't be silly, I don't like eating alone. Janene, I - - -" She looked at him, questioningly. It was he who turned away. "Suit yourself, I don't care one way or another," he said, gruffly.

"That's what I thought," she retorted, turning swiftly away from the door.

"Janene," he called sharply.

"Yes," she answered coolly.

"Dammit, come back here."

"What's the matter?" she asked, anxiously.

"Get this damn tray off my lap, and come here."

She lifted the tray quickly, and sat it on the floor. Then she turned to him questioningly. This time, his eyes did not waver. He grabbed her wrist in a vice-like grip, and pulled her down beside him. She continued to look at him questioningly, but he drew her sharply toward him, his lips claiming hers hungrily. Janene remained passive to begin with, but her resistance melted as his mouth faultlessly continued its task of arousal. Her body ached with exquisite pain as his passion demanded fulfillment in her kiss.

When he released her, he cradled her tightly in his arms, whispering endearments and words of love, which her mind didn't separate into distinct words. Finally, his arms relaxed their hold slightly.

"I love you so much," he whispered, hoarsely. "I don't want to send you away. Please believe that."

She nodded, wordlessly.

"I must. I can't explain fully right now, but you're in danger if I keep you with me." Startled by his words, her body tensed. "No, my love. I'm not in any danger. They won't try to harm me, but they might try to get at me through you, if they ever find out how much you mean to me. That's why I have to send you away. Do you understand?"

She nodded again. "Why didn't you tell me this last night?" she murmured.

"I wanted to, but at the time, I thought the less you knew, the better it would be. But I couldn't stand the hurt in your eyes. I guessed what you were thinking, and I decided that, perhaps, that was best." He tilted her head upward, and kissed her lightly. "I had to hold you in my arms, once more at least, tell you how much I love you, and ask you to wait for me. Will you wait for me?"

Instead of speaking, she pressed her lips to his throat, then raised her head for another kiss.

"No, woman, my breakfast is getting cold."

"You and food," she teased, lightly. "Don't you know you're supposed to be able to live on love alone?"

"Rubbish," he snapped. She replaced the tray across his lap. "Now go get your breakfast and join me." Happily, she hurried downstairs to do his bidding. He was nearly through with his breakfast when he spoke again.

"Janene, I must ask you to do something for me."

"Sure, anything," she agreed readily.

"Anything," he quipped with a wicked gleam.

"Well, almost," she qualified.

"If you truly love me," he began.

"What do you mean, 'if'?" she accused menacingly.

"Poor choice of words," he reflected. "The point is, if anyone should ask you, we met briefly, had a quick affair, and that's it. No one must know that we're engaged, and most of all, that I love you dearly. Do you understand?"

"Yes," she answered. "I might be used to get at you."

"Right."

"Vance, who is 'they', and what's this all about?"

"I can't tell you, as much as I'd like to. It's really

better for us both if you don't know anything. All I ask is that you love me, believe in me, and trust me."

"Is that all?" she said jokingly.

"I've other things in mind," he taunted, suggestively, "but they will come later."

The doorbell chimed.

"That's probably my private nurse," he grimaced.

"I hope she's not pretty," Janene commented.

"Would you be jealous?"

"Yes," she said, bluntly, and hurried to answer the door, leaving him chuckling behind her.

Janene smiled graciously as she opened the door to the mature, austere woman standing on the stoop.

"I'm Mrs. Jennings," she introduced herself. "Dr. Wyatt sent me?"

"I'm Janene Dawson. Your patient is upstairs. I'll take you to him."

Janene introduced the woman to Vance, and showed her the spare room. "I haven't had time to change the sheets," she explained, "but there are plenty in the hall linen closet. I'll change the bed for you, if you like."

"No, that's fine. I can do it myself," the woman answered, as Vance called to Janene.

"I've called your taxi for you. His tab is paid, so don't worry about money. He'll be here in about ten minutes. Kiss me goodbye, but close the door first." She did as she was told, flipped the lock purposefully, and rushed into his open arms.

He kissed her long and hard, then pushed her

gently away. "Get going, will you, before I change my mind."

She unlocked the door, and started out, then turned back. "Your nurse is perfect, don't you think?" she taunted, with a wink.

He threw a pillow at her, which fell harmlessly to the floor at her feet as she sped away.

She had just reached the bottom of the stairs with luggage, when she heard the honking horn of the taxi cab.

"Bye, Vance," she shouted up the stairs, and hurried outside to the waiting cab. As the taxi pulled away from Vance Manor, Janene forced herself not to look back. A curious sense of foreboding settled over her. Deliberately, she made herself think of her last real conversation with Vance, and with a determined breath, expelled her assailing doubts.

# Chapter 11

Janene was glad her work kept her feverishly occupied over the next several days. She was deluged with an overwhelming backlog, which had piled up during her absence. Each night found her falling exhausted into bed with little time to think or wonder about her relationship with the handsome stranger Vance Reeves.

Time passed quickly, and a full ten days had passed before Janene found herself with enough free time to indulge in some reflective thinking. She missed Vance terribly, but had mentally accepted the fact that he did not intend to get in touch with her before he deemed it safe. Her promise to believe in him and trust him she determinedly meant to keep. As the days continued to flee past, she tried firmly to ignore the fact that it had been nearly three weeks since she'd left Vance Manor that morning by taxi.

January led into February and still there was no word at all from Vance. It was an evening in mid-February when she found the suspense intolerable. She had just finished writing a number of letters. Restlessly, she paced her apartment, unable to concentrate either on television, or the novel she had started. She toyed with the idea of writing to Vance, but discarded it as impractical. Finally unable to come to terms with herself, or his silence, she decided to call Vance Manor. It took some time to locate the number, but once she found it, she quickly dialed. She could hear the ringing on the other end of the line, and after the sixth ring, was about to give up, when a male voice answered hesitantly.

"May I speak to Mr. Vance Reeves please?" she asked quickly.

"Mr. Reeves ain't here," the voice answered.

"Could I leave a message?" she asked. There was a pause.

"Don't see much point, ma'am. Mr. Reeves will not be returning. The house is being closed indefinitely. The phone will be disconnected tomorrow."

"Is this Charles?" she asked cautiously.

"Yes, ma'am, and who might you be?" came the abrupt reply.

"This is Janene Dawson. Can you tell me how I can get in touch with Mr. Vance, please?"

"Why, Miss Janene," the voice exclaimed more cordially. "How are you?"

"I'm fine, thank you, Charles. Now, how can I reach Mr. Vance?"

"I'm sorry, I don't know, Miss Janene." A pause followed, while Janene digested this reply, the man continued. "Mr. Vance left over a week ago. He ordered the house closed indefinitely. That's all I know, Miss Janene."

"All right, Charles, thank you," Janene hung up the phone. For several minutes, she sat looking at the instrument. Her thoughts jumbled as she strove to piece the information Charles had given her together. It was useless, Vance apparently had left her no choice but to wait until he chose to contact her. Had this been his intention? Doubts crowded themselves into her unwilling thoughts. Perhaps, he hadn't cared enough for her after all. As she wandered restlessly about the room, Janene tried to come to some conclusion. She recognized at once there was little she could do to force Vance's hand. Either she could go on waiting and hoping until he proved his intentions, or she could make an immediate effort to put him out of her mind and heart. 'Chalk it up to experience, Janene,' she urged herself, pointedly. Wearily, she trudged herself to bed, undecided and unhappy. She spent a fitful night, plagued by dreams in which Vance alternately begged her to believe and trust him, then stood laughing at her as he threw her love back in her face, declaring her a naïve fool.

She awoke the next morning with a headache. Grateful that it was Saturday, she took her time rising. She was unwilling to spend the day alone, and shortly after 9:00 am, called a close friend of hers in Santa Barbara. She made arrangements to drive up and spend the weekend with her friend. They spent time sunning and swimming at the beach; they chatted and shopped, and had dinner at a fantastic seafood restaurant. Deliberately, Janene put all thoughts of Vance out of her mind.

She returned Sunday evening, feeling refreshed and vibrant. She collected her mail and went upstairs to her apartment. She unpacked, showered, and fixed herself a light meal, planning to make it an early night.

Janene had casually tossed the weekend's assortment of mail on the kitchen bar earlier, not bothering even to glance through it.

Now, her evening's tasks completed, she lounged leisurely on the sofa. A cooling breeze stirred the sliding glass door overlooking the small balcony beyond. As she thumbed disinterestedly through the stack of junk mail, she thought casually of writing her parents a brief note before retiring. She was about to heave the entire accumulation of odd shaped circulars and envelopes into the waste can, when a long envelope bearing no return address caught her eye. Her own typewritten address, plus a blurred postmark, were all that adorned the naked envelope. Even the stamp had been dislodged in her shuffle of the particles of mail. Half expecting another advertisement, she tore the envelope open unhurriedly. A single folded newspaper clipping fluttered out and onto her lap.

She picked up the clipping curiously, and unfolded it. Her blue eyes widened in surprise as she gazed at the photo and the bold caption, "Betrothal in the Wind." She painfully recognized the man in the picture at once. It was Vance Reeves, his arm casually about a stunning blonde woman. She quickly searched the envelope for the story that obviously had accompanied the photo. There was none. She examined the envelope again. It revealed no clue as to the sender. She looked at the photo again. There was no doubt in her mind that the man pictured was indeed Vance. He was smiling down warmly at the blonde in his arms. Her face tilted toward his in loving expectation.

Janene crumpled the photo violently, and tossed everything angrily into the nearby wastebasket.

She stood up and took a cigarette from the pack, which had carelessly been tossed on the coffee table. She lit the cigarette and inhaled deeply, expelling the smoke as she walked robot-like out onto the balcony. The cool breeze against her face felt good. She wiped a tear from her cheek absently, as she stared out over the street below, and into the darkness. How long she stood there, she had no idea, but a sudden chill from the night air made her conscious that her thin blue silk peignoir provided little protection from the cold. Slowly, she turned and re-entered the apartment.

Moving in a daze, she checked the locks and turned out the lights. In the darkness, she made her way through the small connecting hall, and into her bedroom. She crawled listlessly between the sheets, lying flat and rigid on one side of the double bed. She willed herself to relax, but her thoughts kept swirling painfully through her mind. It took some time before she reluctantly admitted, and accepted, that the clipping had to have been sent by Vance. He alone knew of their relationship, and only he would know where to send it. As her mind accepted the obvious conclusion, anger asserted itself. She marveled at her own stupidity, her gullible foolishness. Finally, realizing sleep was impossible, she got out of bed. She made her way through the darkened apartment to the kitchen. She turned on the hood light above the stove, and turned on the gas burner under the teakettle. In a few minutes, it was whistling noisily. She quickly made herself a strong cup of instant coffee. Turning off the stove, she sat down at the dinette table, sipping the hot liquid.

Realizing she had to come to terms with her ravaged emotions, she deliberately assessed the relationship she had had with Mr. Vance Reeves. Without a doubt, their brief encounter had left its mark. Gradually, she was able to think of Vance objectively. She found herself gratefully be-laboring the fact that a deeper involvement had been a near miss. It had been cruel of Vance to lead her on, and crueler still to choose this means of throwing her aside. But, at least, she had to admit it was a thorough, clean break. Now, all she had to do was forget him.

At the moment, that seemed an insurmountable task. Long ago, she had decided that no man would ever destroy her life, and she was more determined now than ever that a man would not penetrate her defenses again. She found herself hating Vance for the weaknesses he'd discovered in her armor. Most of all, she was disgusted by what had proved to be her own vulnerability.

An hour later, Janene finally left her solitary retreat, and went to bed. Determinedly, she had shoved Vance Reeves into the hidden recesses of her mind. She had carefully and deliberately planned the course her life would take in the next few months.

# Chapter 12

Janene awoke early. She made coffee and toast, and while eating, wrote a brief, quick letter to her parents. She told them of her decision to resign her job at the end of the summer, and leave California. She would return to Washington in August, be at home for awhile, and decide what and where she would go from there. She offered no other explanation for her decision than that she desired a change. She indicated that she might fulfill the long awaited desire to write for publication.

With the letter finished, Janene quickly dressed for work. Since no one knew of her association with Vance Reeves, there were no sly looks or embarrassing questions to answer. She discovered it surprisingly easy to regulate their brief, torrid affair into the background. Only alone in her apartment, in the evenings, did his vibrant memory assail her, and even that, she discovered, she could fling away at will.

She threw herself into the spring, planning for the summer youth camps she was to organize and staff. After a few tormented weeks, she spent most evenings writing. She began a novel, which was progressing rapidly by the time August rolled around, and she was free to leave the south land.

Her car packed and ready, she experienced no regrets as she handed the key of her apartment to the landlord, and drove northward. She spent a few days with her Santa Barbara friend before going home.

The month of August sped by. She enjoyed the comradeship of family, and by mid-September, her book was on its way to a publisher. Already, she was busy gathering material for a second one. She harbored no illusions. It would be unusual, to say the least, if her book sold immediately, or ever, but she had discovered the fact did not worry her. She knew now that she would keep writing, and eventually, she would be successful.

She had some money saved, and had decided to treat herself to an extended vacation. Her parents had assured her she could stay at home indefinitely, but the eastern Washington cattle ranch, delightful as it was, did not beckon her permanently.

In late September, she took a trip to Seattle, attending a Writer's Conference in that city. There, she met a historical writer named Warren Fielding. Fielding was well-known for his historical writings about his home state of Washington. An avid history enthusiast herself, Janene found the older man fascinating. At their first meeting, they had sat throughout the entire evening in conversation. When the evening came to a close, it had seemed natural for Warren to see her back to her motel. Warren was a stockily built man, in his late forties. He looked like an ex-football player, with graying temples, topped by a thick shock of brown, wavy hair. His eyes were brown, and his bushy eyebrows gave him a sinister appearance. He was not handsome. His ruddy complexion made him appear constantly in a state of over-exertion. Nothing could have been further from the truth. When he was not writing, or researching a project, he was hiking, sailing, or fishing. His vibrant, gregarious personality endeared him to everyone he met. Janene was no exception. During the two-week conference, they saw each other frequently, both at conference related activities, and socially in their free time. There were no romantic overtones to their relationship. They simply liked and enjoyed each other's company, and shared many interests, not only in writing, but in the outdoors, and life in general.

By the time the conference had ended, Janene had agreed to assist Warren Fielding. She would type and transcribe his notes, help him gather research material, and in return, he would help her widen the scope of, and perfect, her own writing skill.

Janene returned home after the conference, happy and eager to embark on what she considered a new career. Even the less-than-enthusiastic acceptance of her plans by her parents did little to dampen her spirits.

Within a fortnight, she had returned to Seattle to take up the threads of a new life. Vance Reeves no longer warranted a fleeting thought.

# Chapter 13

When Janene arrived at Sea-Tac airport, south of Seattle, Warren Fielding was there to meet her. It was a drizzly, cool October Saturday evening. Janene had not expected to be met, although she had notified Fielding of her arrival time, and her intention to report for work on Monday. She had planned to check into a hotel temporarily, until she could find a suitable apartment. She had left her car in eastern Washington, intending to retrieve it, once she had become settled. In the meantime, she'd felt she could manage better without it.

She was somewhat disconcerted when Warren Fielding came hurrying across the terminal to meet her. He greeted her enthusiastically with a bear hug that threatened to collapse her ribcage. Without bothering to ascertain her intentions, he effortlessly grabbed her suitcases, leaving her to follow him bewildered, and bestowed them into the back of his white Mercedes.

Only when she and her belongings were installed in the sleek automobile, and he was competently weaving the automobile from the terminal, did Janene have a chance to ask where they might be headed.

"To my place," he answered, casually.

A sharp intake of breath nearly choked Janene, and she stammered out that she preferred checking into a hotel first.

"Ridiculous," he sputtered. "You'll stay with me,

naturally. No sense in paying for a hotel room when I've plenty of room."

"But," Janene began, flustered. He cast her a quick glance, then began to chuckle. Janene looked at him suspiciously, realizing that she had not made things very clear. She had merely assumed she would have her own place, and report to work on a regular basis. It now appeared she had made some error in her assumption.

Warren was still smiling when she finally recovered enough to speak.

"Warren, I think there's some misunderstanding here. I don't want to go to your place."

"For Heaven's sake, why not?" he asked brusquely. They had stopped at a red light, and he turned to look directly at Janene.

Janene hesitated, searching for the right words, and finally, simply blurted her confusion, saying, "I just don't want to." Then she hurriedly added, "Perhaps I'm not the right person for this job after all."

"Coward," he murmured, studying her carefully, before urging the car forward as the light turned green.

"I am not," she flared, angrily. "I just didn't realize the job was a live-in one, which seems to be what you require."

"And that makes a difference?" he asked. "Why?"

"What do you mean 'why'? That should be obvious. I don't want that kind of relationship."

"What kind of relationship?" he asked, being deliberately obtuse.

Janene was totally confused. She couldn't decide

just where this conversation was leading, but quickly decided she'd had enough. A bus stop loomed ahead. She belatedly wished she'd asked him to drop her there. Instead, she sat stiffly, staring straight ahead, chiding herself for gullibly falling into an awkward situation.

"What kind of relationship do you think I'm offering you, Janene?" he asked, quietly, after she had remained silent for several minutes. She did not answer. Abruptly, he pulled the car to the curb, and turned off the ignition. She avoided his eyes, but he reached across to secure her chin gently between his thumb and forefinger, and turning her head, so he could see her eyes.

"I don't know what that vivid little imagination of yours has cooked up in that pretty little head. I'm not suggesting anything, nor am I carrying you off to an old man's den of iniquity. I have a January 1st deadline to meet on my next book, which at the moment, is barely started. I need someone to help with that project. Now, do you want the job or not?"

"Yes, I do," Janene decided, spontaneously. "I think it offers me the writing experience I'd take years to observe and learn otherwise."

"Fine, that's settled. Shall we go?"

"I guess so, but I still don't understand why I can't stay at a hotel," she insisted.

"You could, but it is absolutely pointless. I have a large house on Lake Washington, complete with a housekeeper and other domestic staff. I've had prepared a suite of rooms for your own use. You'll have all the privacy you want, plus you'll be close to the work required. I'm afraid I don't work on a scheduled timetable. Sometimes I work all night, sometimes during the day, and more often than not, not at all. It would simply be more convenient for me to have you on the premises."

"I see," Janene murmured, though in reality, she was more confused than ever. But she offered no further comment. She relaxed outwardly, willing herself to withhold further discussion until she had had a chance to assess the situation more thoroughly. She was unsure just what she had expected, and realized that perhaps she ought to have discussed the aspects of the job more thoroughly before making a commitment.

They pulled into the circular drive of a huge colonial-styled mansion. Although it was quite dark, the immaculate grounds were well lit. A door light revealed giant pillars of what appeared to be a veranda.

The door opened as the car halted, and a man emerged quickly.

"Good evening, Mr. Fielding," he said, solicitously.

"Good evening, Sam. This is Miss Dawson. Take her bags to the East wing, and then put the car away."

"Very good, Sir."

Warren Fielding guided Janene's hesitant footsteps up the steps to the front door, his hand lightly grasping her elbow.

The entrance opening into a large entryway was flanked on one side by a closet, the other by mirrors. They passed through this to view an enormous sunken living room, from which a grand carpeted stairway led to the upper levels. To the left was a formal dining room, beyond which were doors that no doubt led to the kitchen. Janene was awe struck. Never had she been in such a massively sized house.

A middle-aged woman came bustling through the dining room, wiping her hands lightly on her apron. She greeted them, and taking their coats, hung them in the entry closet.

"Sarah Jane, this is Janene Dawson. You will please show her to her rooms."

"How do you do, Miss. If you will follow me, please," the woman greeted Janene warmly.

"Janene," Warren called, as she moved toward the stairway. "Freshen up, then join me here in fifteen minutes. How soon until dinner, Sarah Jane?"

"About forty minutes, sir," came the reply.

"Fine, that will give us time for a cocktail."

Janene nodded, and followed the maid up the carpeted stairway to the next landing. Here, the landing merged into a hall leading in both directions. The maid led Janene to the right, past several closed doors. The door she opened led into a roomy sitting room, complete with fireplace and television. They passed through this into an enormous bedroom, furnished in heavy turn-of-the-century oak furniture. Janene saw her cases sitting on a rack at the foot of the double bed. Besides the bed, there was a massive dresser, two nightstands, a window seat, and an occasional chair. The maid threw open another door, indicating a bathroom, and dressing room.

"There is also a half-kitchenette off the other

end of the sitting room," she said. "I hope you will find everything to your satisfaction, Miss."

"I'm sure I will, thank you."

"Will that be all, Miss? Would you like me to help you unpack?"

"No, that won't be necessary. Thank you."

The maid slipped out then, closing the door.

Janene looked about, amazed. When Warren said a suite of rooms, he had meant just that. She opened her cases, but decided to forego unpacking for the moment. She walked into the dressing room, smiling as she thought how lonesome her meager wardrobe would be hanging in its vastness. She went through to the bathroom, which contained an enormous sunken tub, with a shower and, of course, a toilet. One side of the dressing room contained two marble-topped sinks, backed by a full mirror. Quickly, she washed her hands and applied fresh lipstick. With a few deft strokes, she brushed her hair, then deciding she would be more comfortable without her suit jacket, removed it. Her bright, multicolored lavender blouse enhanced the blue of her eyes, giving them a slightly violet tinge. Her black, slim skirt displayed a trim figure, and slender legs. She walked back through the bedroom into the sitting room. It, too, contained antique furniture. There was a small high-backed settee, two straight-backed velvet occasional chairs, and a small drop-leaf writing desk. A large fireplace covered one end of the room, and a portable TV completed the furnishings. She moved across the room and pushed the lowered swinging door, which revealed a well-equipped modern kitchenette. No apartment would ever match this for luxury, she noted, as she pushed aside sliding doors to reveal a washer and dryer. One side of the room was encased in drapes. As she pulled the cord to reveal what was beyond, a squeal of delight escaped her lips. There were sliding glass doors leading to a small balcony. The view was breathtaking. It looked out over the lake, simmering with twinkling lights of other nearby residences. An array of small lights glimmered as stars in the distance. She could visualize Mount Rainier in the distance, though, of course, she could not actually see it in the darkness.

Glancing at her watch, she was suddenly alerted that she'd spent twenty minutes exploring, and hurriedly, she left the room to re-join Warren, who awaited her downstairs.

She did not immediately see Warren Fielding as she stepped into the sunken living room. He was hidden from view by a walled partition that flanked one side of the stairway. His back was toward her as he stood gazing out the window, a drink in his hand.

He turned as he heard her approach, and moved toward the bar. "What would you like?" he asked.

"A White Cadillac," she answered.

He nodded, and quickly mixed the vodka and crème de cocoa. He placed the drink in her hand, and waited politely for her to seat herself on one of the two pink Cleopatra chairs. She sat down rather stiffly on the foot of the chair, wishing immediately she had chosen someplace else. Her eyes quickly noted the room and its furnishings. A large baby grand piano sat in the corner, flanked by huge bay windows with window seats on each side. There was a sofa with wooden legs, a couple of occasional tables, the two Cleopatra chairs, and two more straight-backed occasional chairs. A bookcase and writing table sat along the entry wall. It was an uncomfortable-looking room, and Janene felt uncomfortable.

"Rather a disaster, I agree," Warren perceptively analyzed her gaze.

Janene flushed.

"Don't be embarrassed," he added. "I had nothing to do with these furnishings, and I don't generally use this room. Suppose we retire to the den until dinner?" With that, he pushed the bar to which he had prepared their drinks. Janene watched in pure amazement as the entire bar retreated into the wall, leaving only the blank wall exposed. It was then she noticed the doorway beyond. She arose and followed him into the adjoining room. It, too, was large: leather chairs and sofa, ringing a blazing fireplace, looked definitely more inviting. The bar, fully exposed, was now in this room. She seated herself on the sofa, her eyes on the fire. He stood leaning casually against the mantel.

"What do you think of my home?" he asked, quietly.

"Well, it's something else again," she answered honestly.

"That's a vague reply, if I ever heard one," he chuckled. "It is a bit ostentatious and overwhelming, isn't it?" he added. "Actually, I bought it lock, stock, and barrel, so to speak. Since I don't spend a lot of time here myself,

I've only bothered to modernize a few of the rooms. The others I've left pretty much original. The living room is an example. It's really ghastly."

Janene laughed. "I agree, it's pretty awful, despite all that beautiful antique furniture."

"That's just it, antiquated as hell," he commented drily.

Silence fell between them as he re-filled their glasses.

Abruptly, he asked, "What makes you so wary of men, Janene?"

"I didn't know that I was," she replied vaguely.

"You are, definitely. I had the distinct feeling you had me pegged as some sort of lecher earlier."

"I'm sorry about that," Janene apologized. "I was just surprised, that's all. I hadn't realized you planned that I should live here. I had expected to rent an apartment, and once settled in, bring my car over. I didn't mean to be rude."

"You drive, then."

She nodded. "I'll put a car at your disposal, and feel free to use it whenever you like."

"That really isn't necessary," she insisted, hastily.

"It comes with the job," he remarked, casually. "I shall be requiring a good deal of research, and you will often have to go to the library, or elsewhere, to get it. Our city transit system leaves a great deal to be desired, in many respects. You haven't asked about salary."

"I have no idea what the job I do is worth, so I can't very well estimate my worth."

He named the figure he intended paying her, plus an expense account for gasoline and food, should she have to eat out while researching, the car, and, of course, board and room. She found it more than generous, and said so.

He dismissed her arguments completely, so she gracefully gave in, mentally calculating that she could save practically all of her salary.

"The job will last through January. After that, depending on how well we work together, my next commission, etc., well, it could extend much longer. Does that suit you?"

"Yes," she answered quietly. At that moment, the maid entered to announce dinner. Warren escorted her into the dining room. The table set for two. The meal was simple, but well prepared, consisting of roast beef, salad, rolls, and vegetables. For dessert, there was a lush deep-dish apple pie.

After dinner, they retired to the den for their coffee. Janene soon found events of the day catching up with her, and she barely stifled a yawn.

Warren talked about the work he hoped they could accomplish in the ensuing week. Noticing Janene's stifled yawn, he asked indulgently, "Are you tired?"

"I am rather," she admitted. "I think I'd just better go to bed."

"You do that, and rest well, goodnight, Janene."

"Goodnight, Warren." Janene arose, and was about to leave the room, when his voice halted.

"Janene," he said, softly.

"Yes."

"I hope we can be friends, as well as co-workers."

"I'm sure we can, Warren, and thank you," she smiled warmly, as she met his gaze confidently.

"Do you have any plans for tomorrow?" he asked.

"Not really," she admitted, realizing that she need no longer look for an apartment.

"I'm going sailing tomorrow. Would you like to come along?" he asked.

"I'd love to," she agreed, without hesitation, her earlier suspicions forgotten.

"Fine, I'll see you tomorrow, then. Goodnight, Janene."

"Goodnight," she re-iterated, and climbed the stairs, wearily. She had not unpacked, but decidedly she took her nightgown from one of the cases, and left the rest packed for another time. She was simply too tired to care.

# Chapter 14

The weeks passed quickly. Warren Fielding was a relentless taskmaster. Janene found little time to work on her own writing. Though the work was demanding, she enjoyed every minute. On weekends, she and Warren went out sailing, or spent the time together, enjoying a variety of other activities. He took her to historical sites, and museums; they visited local Indian villages, they had even flown to Washington, D.C. to visit the Archives. Their relationship remained purely platonic, one of good friends, nothing more. Janene sensed this was more due to her attitude toward Warren, and other men, than to Warren's efforts. Nevertheless, she wanted it that way, and Warren had made no personal demands upon her, and for this, she was grateful. She knew she cared for him deeply, but she did not see a future in a deeper relationship than friendship. Vance Reeves rarely crossed her mind these days, and for that, too, she was thankful.

It was two weeks before Christmas when it suddenly dawned on her how quickly time had elapsed.

Warren had scheduled a Saturday trip to the Ezra Meeker Mansion in Puyallup, but Janene had decided to beg off. She had Christmas shopping to do, and she was a bit weary of weekend excursions. She was disturbed by Warren's decision to forego the trip himself when she altered her plans.

She was surprised to find him ready to drive her

downtown Saturday morning. She insisted it wasn't necessary, but when he confessed to having shopping to do, also, she reluctantly agreed.

As usual, Janene found Warren an amiable companion. After parking the car in the South Center Shopping Mall lot, and agreeing to meet her for lunch at one o'clock in a nearby restaurant, Warren took off on his own.

Left to her own devices, and undecided about purchases for those on her Christmas list, Janene spent most of the morning browsing through the crowded shops of the Mall. She detested shopping of any kind, especially during the holiday rush. She had been too busy during the past weeks to follow her usual practice of making a list of possible gift items for each person on her Christmas list. Thwarted, she found it impossible to make adequate selections. By one o'clock, she had managed to purchase two books for herself, delicate scarves and boxes of cigars for the members of Warren's domestic staff, but the bulk of her shopping still remained incomplete. Tired and disgruntled, she made her way back through the ever increasing crowds to the restaurant where she was to meet Warren.

He was waiting for her at a table near the window, absently sipping a drink. She slid wearily into the booth seat opposite him. He ordered a drink for her, and another for himself, requesting a luncheon menu.

He looked at the half-dozen parcels she placed on the seat beside her, and grinned.

"I take it you're not finished," was his mild comment.

"Lord, no," she retorted waspishly. "I haven't really started, and I've walked miles. My feet are killing me. I hate shopping anyway, and what's worse, I can't seem to make up my mind what to get anybody. And you?"

"I'm finished," he said, smugly.

"Do you know I hate you?" she said, with a grimace.

"Figured you might," he grinned.

Janene ordered a chef salad, and Warren had barbecued spare ribs. They ate leisurely, their conversation general and uninhibited. It was nearly two-thirty when they rose to go.

"Look, Warren," Janene said, as they emerged onto the enclosed mall center. "There's no use of you waiting around here for me. I'll finish my shopping, and take a taxi back."

"You'll do no such thing. Give me those parcels, and I'll put them in the car, then I'll help you. An indecisive female needs the assistance of a domineering, decisive male. Now, you stay put right here until I get back," he ordered, taking her parcels, calling over his shoulder as he departed, "Besides, I'm excellent at carrying packages." Janene giggled, calling after him, "Idiot."

As the afternoon progressed, Janene marveled at his patience. He actually seemed to enjoy the shopping, and offered countless suggestions, which helped speed up her shopping immensely. By five o'clock, she had finally finished, except for one gift. That, she decided, would have to wait until another time, as it was a gift for Warren. At first, she had been undecided about getting him anything. At last, she'd concluded that she'd buy something to show her appreciation for his kindness. She wasn't expecting anything from him, but she'd feel better knowing she had something for him in reserve. She could always give it to one of her brothers, or return it, if she decided later not to give it to him. The trouble was, she hadn't the remotest idea what sort of gift to get.

Miraculously, the decision was made for her, when on the return trip, Warren stopped at a nautical supply shop. He wanted to purchase some replacement fishing tackle. Although she was extremely weary, and the thought of more shopping gave her a headache, she accompanied him into the shop.

She knew nothing of fishing equipment, so left him alone to make his selections, while she wandered aimlessly around the shop. Accidently, she stumbled on to some seamen's clothing. A Norwegian fishnet sweater took her eye. Making sure that Warren was occupied, she purchased the sweater along with a seaman's cap, labeled "Skipper." In addition, she purchased a guidebook of sailing points in and about the San Juan Islands. In her frequent sailings with Warren, she had noted he never dressed the part, nor did he seem to possess any books on sailing, even though he was a seasoned sailor.

Leaving her parcels on the counter, she crossed to the aisle in which he still stood studying various fishing gear. She told him she was going back to the car to wait, as her feet hurt.

He nodded absently, then told her he wouldn't be much longer. Quickly, she returned to the counter, retrieved her packages, and hastily left for the car. Carefully, bestowing the parcels with the rest in the back seat of the car, she climbed in front to wait.

She was almost asleep when, some twenty minutes later, Warren returned to the car. They rode in silence, Janene half-dozing.

Warren drove straight to the garage, parking the car within the garage himself. Laden with packages, they entered the house through the kitchen entrance. Warren followed her upstairs to her sitting room, where they deposited their load on the settee. Then Warren returned to the car for the remainder. A few minutes later, he was back with another armful. This, too, was added to the pile. He then flopped down in mock fatigue in an occasional chair, legs stretched before him.

Janene smiled at his exaggeration; removing her coat, she went into the dressing room. She kicked off her pumps, and slipped into a pair of soft mules, washing her hands before returning to the sitting room.

She was somewhat surprised to find Warren exactly as she'd left him, sprawled in the chair.

"Are you hungry?" he asked.

"Not particularly," she replied.

"Good, because I'd forgotten until now that I gave Sarah the weekend off, so if we eat, we either go out, or fix it ourselves."

"I'm really not hungry, Warren, and besides, I

couldn't make it to the car if my life depended on it," she answered, tiredly, as she sank into the other chair.

"You have any eggs and milk?" he asked, casually.

"Yes, I think so, why?"

"Well, I make a pretty mean omelette. Why don't you make some coffee, and I'll whip us up an omelette," he suggested.

"Fine," she agreed.

He slipped off his coat, and tossed it atop the parcels as he rose and headed for the kitchenette. Janene followed quickly. She made a percolator of coffee, then perched on a kitchen stool, and watched as he whipped eggs, milk and grated cheese together.

In a few minutes, they were eating a delicious omelette, and drinking hot coffee. The kitchenette possessed only two stools at a narrow bar.

"You cooked, I'll wash up," Janene said, when they had finished. Warren nodded, and left her to it. She heard the television come on in the next room, and warily wondered when he intended to go back downstairs. She finished the clearing up, then joined Warren in the sitting room. He was sitting with his feet on the hassock, watching the news. She cleared off the settee, arranging the packages in a pile against the wall. Then she, too, sat down. For awhile, they watched television companionably. Janene could not keep from yawning. It was after ten when Warren arose saying, "I've got to get going. You're tired, aren't you, honey?" he said, using the endearment unconsciously. Janene nodded, trying vainly to stifle another yawn. Warren picked up his coat, and headed for the door.

Janene followed him. "Thanks, Warren. You were really great today, and I appreciate it."

"Aren't I always?" he teased, softly turning so suddenly that Janene collided with him.

His hands on her shoulders steadied her as she regained her balance. She looked up at him, seeing a tenderness in his eyes that she'd never noticed before. She dropped her gaze, but instead of releasing her, he dropped one arm to encircle her waist, while his other hand tilted her chin to force her eyes to meet his intent gaze. His lips covered hers unhurriedly, their pressure increasing, as in surprise, her own lips parted beneath his. Abruptly, the kiss ended, and he drew away, his eyes never leaving her face. Then he turned, as the door closed sharply behind him.

Puzzled and dismayed, Janene stared at the closed door. "Oh, God," she thought, despairingly, not again. She enjoyed their casual relationship so much, and in nearly two months of working and playing together, Warren had not once made a pass at her until tonight. Fervently, she hoped it would not change their friendship. She liked Warren immensely, but she knew she could not think of him in that way. For the first time in several weeks, Vance Reeves haunted her memory as she slept fitfully that night.

# Chapter 15

She didn't see Warren the following day. She breakfasted in her room, then did her laundry, and wrote some Christmas letters. It was afternoon before she ventured downstairs. Warren had left a note for Sarah Jane on the kitchen table. Feeling much like she was eaves-dropping, she had read its crypt message stating that he would not be back until late, so would not be expecting dinner, and informing Sarah Jane she should check to see if Miss Dawson would need anything.

Curiously, she wondered why he had not mentioned a trip last night, as evidently he had left before she was up.

The house was so big and empty that Janene became restless, and decided to attend a movie. She quickly scribbled a post-script to the note Warren had left, telling Sarah Jane she would eat her evening meal out. She decided against taking Warren's second car that she used regularly. Instead, she walked to the bus stop, and took the bus.

The house was dark when she returned that evening. Either Sarah Jane had retired early, or had not returned. It was, also, obvious that Warren was not yet back. There was a light in Sam's quarters above the garage, but that was all. She let herself quietly in the front door, and headed immediately toward the stairway leading to her room. She knew it was not yet eight o'clock, but it had been dark for some time.

She was about half-way across the living room, not having turned on a light, when she saw the figure silhouetted against the far window. A scream rose to her throat, and stuck. The next thing she knew, someone was patting her face with stinging slaps, repeating her name.

"Janene, Janene, for God's sake, darling, what's the matter?"

Her eyes fluttered unwillingly against the blazing glare of the lights. Slowly, her eyes recognized Warren's kneeling figure. She quivered uncontrollably, and forceful arms lifted her and laid her gently on the sofa.

"You damn little fool. Why didn't you turn on a light? You could have killed yourself on those stairs with a fall like that."

"I didn't fall," she snapped, hotly.

"No, I suppose you were just taking a nap on the floor," he rasped, caustically.

"You don't need to be so nasty," she replied, contritely. "I was crossing the room to the stairway when I saw this man silhouetted against that window. I was scared spitless. I tried to scream, but I couldn't. I don't know what happened then."

Sudden comprehension showed in Warren's face as he said quietly, "You must have fainted. It was me at the window. I heard a door open and close, then a third noise and when I turned on the light, I found you in a crumpled heap at the foot of the stairs. My God, I thought you'd fallen down the stairs. I didn't realize it was the front door I heard. I must have aged ten years when I saw you lying there," he continued, running a hand agitatedly through his hair.

"And you yell at me for not turning on a light," she giggled. "What ever were you doing standing there in the dark?" she asked, sitting up and swinging her legs to the floor.

"I was trying to work up some courage, I guess," Warren answered, dejectedly.

"Courage?" Janene repeated, stupidly.

"Yes, dammit, courage. Is that so hard to understand?" he snapped.

"No, I guess not, but why?"

"To ask you to marry me," he murmured, huskily, turning away from the stunned expression on her face. "No, don't say anything yet. Just hear me out, please. When I met you at the conference, I knew you were the woman I'd been searching for all my life. I, also, knew I was practically old enough to be your father. Nevertheless, I knew I couldn't just let you walk away. I felt if I confessed my feelings too soon, it would scare you off, so I offered you a job. I planned to take my time, win your respect and confidence, and maybe, eventually, your love. I botched the entire thing last night. We'd had such a wonderful day together, and somehow, I didn't want it to end." He paused, his back still turned toward her.

"You created this job especially for me, didn't you, Warren?" she asked, quietly.

"Yes and no. I do have a January 1st deadline to meet. I've managed to extend until the 31st, but that was the truth. Usually, I hire a team of researchers at various libraries throughout the country, and I do much of the research myself. After all the data is collected, I hole up for a month or two, and write the work. Then it is sent to a typist, and to the publisher. I delayed this project longer than usual. Your interest and enthusiasm displayed during the conference gave me the idea that we could do this project together. I'm convinced that through your efforts, it will be my best work. I've always considered myself a confirmed bachelor, that is, until I met you. Then, suddenly, I found I wanted and needed someone to share my life, and my work. I've been driving around all day trying to decide whether I should ask you to marry me or not. I love you very much, Janene, and I'll do everything in my power to make you happy." His voice was husky with emotion. He turned to face her now.

She lifted her eyes to meet his tormented gaze.

"I'm sorry," she murmured, softly.

"I know, you don't love me. You care for me, but it isn't love. I don't care. I've enough for both of us. I know that some man hurt you deeply. I hate him for that, but in a way, I'm grateful. He's made you wary and distrustful of men. You don't react that way toward me, and I know that given time, I could make you love me."

"I wish it worked that way, Warren. But you can't make a person love you. I'd never feel good about it. I'd feel I was cheating you."

"I don't care," he said, emotionally. "I love you, and just having you near me is enough."

"For how long?" she asked. "There's no need to

answer that. You're willing to take a chance. I'm not. I don't want to be married to a man that might someday become suspicious, jealous, even grow to hate me because he knew from the start I didn't love him. I'd give anything if I did love you, Warren, but I don't. I'm sorry."

A heavy silence fell between them. Slowly, Janene got to her feet.

"I suppose you'll be leaving now?" he asked.

"Don't you want me to?" came the soft reply.

"No."

"But it's the best thing all around."

"For whom? You or me?" he asked, gruffly. She did not answer, so he continued. "I'd like you to forget this conversation ever took place. I still need to meet my deadline, and I need your help more than ever to do that. I want you to stay until this project is completed. After that, you're free to go or stay as you like. I promise to keep the relationship business-like and impersonal. This doesn't mean I'm giving up, Janene. I still intend to try to win your love, and I don't care how long it takes. Who knows, maybe one day you'll need me. I'll bide my time. Right now, I desperately need your help, and I want you to stay."

Janene looked at him helplessly, not knowing quite what to say or do. She searched his eyes for a clue, but saw only the gentle concern they'd always held for her. A long silence ensued as she turned away from his penetrating gaze.

"All right, Warren. I'll stay," she said, hesitantly, "but only until this project is finished. I will leave for home on the 22nd, and I'll be back on the 27th. Once this writing is finished, I'll be leaving for good."

"Fine, we've got approximately ten days to complete the final research. During your absence, I'll complete the first draft. By the end of January, or before, the work will be finished. I won't try to hold you then. Agreed?"

"Agreed," she answered, and left him standing there, his eyes following her longingly, mirroring the pain he felt inside.

Janene had prepared herself for an awkward morning. Though he looked tired and drawn, he made no reference to their conversation the day before. She soon realized from the start of information he asked her to verify, that he had probably worked all night. She spent the next three days in the public library seeing little of Warren. On Thursday and Friday, she transcribed pages of material from the dictaphone. He was so far ahead of her that she worked most of Saturday as well. Warren was gone all weekend. She did not ask where, and he did not offer the information. She worked feverishly through Wednesday, and that evening, Warren drove her to the airport. She had not wanted him to, but he'd insisted. As she was boarding the plane, he slipped a small package into her hand.

"Merry Christmas," he had said, brushing his lips across hers lightly. Her flight was called then. He strode off quickly, without a backward glance. She looked at the package in her hand and dashed to a nearby phone. Quickly, she dialed the Fielding residence. When Sarah Jane answered, she told her where the presents she had gotten Warren were, and asked her to leave them in some conspicuous place for him Christmas Eve. She'd already given the staff their gifts, but had not known whether to go ahead and give Warren his. She hung up the phone and ran up the corridor as the loud speaker called her flight for the last and final time.

She opened the package on the plane, not wanting to explain its contents to her family. It was a lovely ruby ring, flanked by two miniature diamonds. She realized at once that Warren had undoubtedly chosen it as an engagement ring. Tears filled her eyes, for she knew intuitively that he'd wanted her to have it despite the fact that she'd rejected his proposal. It was an expensive gift, and one she ordinarily wouldn't accept. However, she couldn't hurt Warren more, knowing as she did that he wanted her to have it in any case.

She slipped the ring into its delicate case, and put it in her purse. She would wear it after Christmas, when she returned to him.

# Chapter 16

It was still early evening when Janene's flight touched down at Yakima Municipal Airport. Her younger brother and his wife were there to meet her. In just over an hour they were gathered in the big ranch house that was the center of the Dawson ranch.

Much later, after the family had dispersed to their own various homes, Janene was finally alone in the room that had been hers since girlhood. She was extremely tired, the tension of the last few weeks gone, leaving her totally exhausted. She undressed, took a long shower, preparing for bed. She glanced at the stack of collected mail her mother had given her, debating upon whether to tackle it tonight. Fairly certain it was mostly Christmas mail, she decided there was no harm in going through it before retiring. Any letters she could leave until later to read.

Sorting abstractedly through the pile, she sat aside personal letters, threw junk mail into the wastebasket, gathering only a few envelopes together for immediate attention.

She yawned wearily as she opened the third envelope. Suddenly her eyes widened, sleepiness vanishing, and she dashed downstairs, shouting, "Mom and Dad, I did it!" Her eyes were dancing with excitement as she waved the letter frantically above her head.

"What on earth is the matter, Janene?" her mother

asked, calmly coming out of the bedroom, tying her robe and searching for her glasses. Her father followed.

"I've done it, I've done it," Janene shouted wildly. "Look."

She handed a piece of paper to her Dad.

"Why, it's a check for $2,000," he exclaimed. "It's made out to you?" he continued, thoughtfully.

"That's right, they've bought my book. It's going to be published in January. Isn't it wonderful?"

"It certainly is," her mother's voice agreed. She didn't sound excited, but her eyes were glowing warmly.

"So my daughter's a famous author," her Dad smiled, as he handed the check back to her.

"Well, not famous yet, but I'm on my way," she laughed, hugging them both. "I can't believe it. My first book, and not even a rejection slip."

"I thought you were tired," her father remarked indulgently.

"I was, but I'm not now. I'm so excited and happy, I'm about to burst," she exclaimed, dancing around joyously.

"Nevertheless, it's past one o'clock, and I think we'd all better get to bed," her father's stern voice ordered, though his eyes tempered the demand.

"Okay, dad," Janene smiled affectionately, "but I won't be able to sleep." Nevertheless, she started up the stairs, calling "goodnight" as she left them.

In her own room once more, she re-read the publisher's letter, forgetting all about the rest of her mail. Dreamily, she sat on the edge of the bed. "I'm a writer," she thought, ecstatically. "And they want to see more manuscripts." Her problems completely forgotten, Janene turned out the light and crawled in bed. Almost instantly, she was sound asleep, a faint smile of happiness clinging to her soft lips.

The next few days were a bustle of excited activity. Christmas came and went. All too soon it was time for Janene to return to Seattle. Once her job with Warren was completed, she'd hoped to plunge herself fully into writing. Thanks to Warren, and the publishing of her book, her bank balance was healthy enough to allow her to do just that.

She had not told Warren exactly when she'd return, not wanting him to meet her. She had put his ring on. It twinkled on her left hand brazenly. She had intended to wear it on her right hand, but it hadn't fit properly, so after some deliberation, finally placed it on her third finger, left hand, which she knew was where he had intended for it to go.

Much of the flight back she had seriously mulled over the prospect of his proposal. Although nothing had been said since that night, she instinctively knew that he'd ask her again. At times, it almost seemed to be the answer to everything. Married to Warren, she'd have time and money to pursue her own writing career. Furthermore, they got along well together, and shared so many interests. 'But can you marry a man you don't really love?' she asked herself over and over. She chided herself for wanting too much from life, and by the time the plane landed at Sea-Tac Airport, her mind was in a complete mass of confusion.

She was thoroughly dismayed, and searched wildly for a means of escape, when she saw Warren Fielding waiting at the terminal gate for her.

It took all her inner strength to walk calmly toward him. She felt self-conscious and gauche.

He greeted her with a warming, friendly smile. "Have a good time?" he asked, casually, as they walked toward the baggage area.

"Wonderful, and I've some really exciting news," she said shyly.

"I thought you looked unusually animated and happy," he commented, taking the baggage check she handed him.

She watched him walk away with mixed emotions. He was really such a dear, she thought.

She had become absorbed in watching a young mother trying to cope with an obstreperous two-year-old boy, luggage, and a baby, and she was not aware of Warren's approach until he spoke.

"She looks a little frantic," he remarked, following her gaze. "I think she could use some help." With that, he placed Janene's case at her feet, and walked toward the young woman.

He said something to her, which she received with a grateful smile, then effortlessly he hoisted the squirming mass of humanity into one arm, grabbing her suitcase in his other hand. Within minutes, he had the young woman, her charges, and belongings, installed in a nearby cab, and was waving them off.

When he re-joined her, Janene said, "That was a nice thing to do."

"I'm a nice guy, in case you hadn't noticed," he answered lightly, as he led the way to his car.

As he opened the car door for her, he caught her left hand in a rough clasp, his eyes on the ring he'd given her.

"Did you like it?" he asked softly.

She met his gaze hesitantly, but her voice was steady.

"I love it. It's really beautiful. Thank you."

Impulsively, she raised on tiptoe and kissed his cheek lightly. His ruddy color deepened as he looked about in embarrassment. He closed the door as she settled into the front seat.

As he started the car, she spoke again. "I really shouldn't accept it, you know. It's far too expensive a gift. It wouldn't fit on any other finger, so I had to wear it here." Realizing she was just chattering needlessly, she stopped abruptly.

"It's where it belongs," he stated drily, confirming her suspicions that he'd intended it to be an engagement ring.

"Are you hungry?" he asked casually, changing the topic of conversation.

"I could probably eat. Why?"

"I thought we'd stop some place for dinner – Sarah Jane is off for a few days. Her sister became very ill just before Christmas. She probably won't be back for another week. I've been batching, so the house is rather in a mess, I'm afraid. I made reservations at the Space Needle Restaurant. Is that okay with you?"

"Fine, how did you know when I'd come in?" she asked curiously.

"Well, there aren't many flights from Yakima, so it wasn't hard to check," he grinned.

They were nearly finished with their dinner when Warren asked, "What's the exciting news?"

"I've sold my book," she exclaimed.

"Well, congratulations. So you're a full-fledged authoress now," he said with genuine pleasure.

She told him all about her book sale, and they lingered over coffee.

Finally, Warren picked up the check and arose. He guided her through the tables, and in a few minutes, they were headed for his place.

They entered through the kitchen, and Janene took mental stock of the clutter, vowing to do something about it in the morning.

Although it wasn't late, Janene decided to call it a day. She was preparing to climb the stairs to her rooms when Warren spoke.

"How about sharing a night cap with me?"

"I don't think so. I think I'll just unpack, shower, and call it a night," she answered.

"Don't go yet. The house has been pretty empty these last few days. At least take pity on me, and keep me company for a little while."

She turned toward him, but his back was to her. The bar was open, and she could see that he was mixing himself a rather stiff drink.

"All right, but only for a little while," she answered.

"Yes, that's fine." She walked past him, and into the den, seating herself on the sofa.

He brought their drinks, closed the bar, and touched a match to the carefully stacked logs in the fireplace. It was soon roaring. He had made no attempt at conversation, and neither did she.

"I liked your gifts," he said, quietly turning toward her, and taking the glass from her hand. He sat it down. Unsure of his intentions, Janene allowed him to take her hands and pull her to her feet.

"This is my thanks," he said, softly drawing her to him, and placing a firm kiss on her unresisting lips. Then, roughly, he pulled her into his arms, burying his head in the silky softness of her hair.

"God, I missed you," he whispered hoarsely, his arms tightening in their embrace. She turned her head away from him, and his lips touched her throat tenderly.

"Warren, don't do this," she pleaded, struggling to break his hold.

"I can't help myself," he choked emotionally, turning her head so his lips found hers in a crushing, bruising kiss, releasing the pent up passion within him. Janene allowed her body to go limp, passively accepting his demanding lips. As his arms relaxed, she quickly broke away.

She stared at him, watching the blazing passion

in his eyes die, knowing how much her lack of response hurt him. His arms hung limply at his sides, his shoulders sagged in defeat as he turned from her.

"I'll pack my things. I'll find a hotel for tonight, and send for the rest of my things tomorrow," she said, calmly, her voice belying the torn emotions inside.

"You don't need to go, Janene," he said brokenly. "I never meant to behave like this. I'm truly sorry. It won't happen again."

"I really think it's best I go."

"Well, I don't," he said sharply. "You made me a promise, and by God, you'll keep it."

"I can't stay here after this," she said, jerkily.

"You can, and what's more, you will. The book will be finished by the 31st. After that, you can go, but not before. There isn't time to replace you now, and they won't give me an extension. Either I finish it or chuck it, and I don't propose to do the latter. I should have let you walk out that first night, but I didn't. Now I can't afford to let you go." His voice was harsh and cold, with anger. His tone sent a shiver along Janene's spine. She had known he was tough, but this was a side of his character she'd never witnessed before. She wasn't sure how to proceed. Logic told her he could not force her to stay, but in this mood, he might try. She was not up to that kind of a scene.

When next he spoke, his voice was controlled. She could sense the smoldering anger still, but she could not be certain if it was directed at her or at himself.

"The situation between us is one of my own creation. God knows you've given me no encouragement. The hell of it is, I can't help the way I feel about you any more than you can help how you feel. It's my problem, and I'm stuck with it. I don't expect to ever be quite the same again, but I'll live. It's my private hell, and if I prefer the torture of having you near me, it's no concern of yours."

"I'm sorry," Janene murmured. "I wish I'd never taken this job."

"So do I," he stated, grimly. Seeing her stricken face, his voice became gentler.

"Don't worry about me, my love. One doesn't die of a broken heart, you know. I took my chances, and I lost. You've been nothing but honest with me. Just help me finish this damn assignment. Surely you owe me that much."

"All right, Warren, if that's the way you want it. I guess I do owe you that much consideration."

"That's my girl," he said, gruffly.

"It's funny," she said, reflectively.

"What is?"

"Someone once told me there could never be friendship between a man and a woman, only love or hate. I didn't believe that until now. I thought you and I could be friends, were friends. Why does it have to be this way?"

"I don't know. I honestly did not set out to fall in love with you. We'll always be friends, and I mean that."

"I'm so sorry, Warren. I wish things could be different."

"So do I, love, but as I said before, neither of us can

help the way we feel." He chuckled drily. "I'd probably make a damn lousy husband anyway."

"I don't think so," Janene disagreed, sincerely. She had taken the second drink he held out to her. She just sat staring into the fire. A heavy silence had fallen between them. Miles away, Janene toyed with her half-filled glass.

"What makes you look so sad? Have I caused that?" Warren asked gently, bringing Janene abruptly back to the present.

"Oh, no," she assured him. "I was thinking of someone else entirely."

"The man who hurt you?" he questioned perceptively. She nodded. "Would you like to talk about it?" She remained thoughtful, wondering if telling Warren about Vance, sharing her disillusionment and misery with him, might help to exorcise Vance from her system. At the same time, she wondered if it was fair to Warren, did he deserve hearing about the man she loved, especially now? For had she never met Vance, might she have been able to return Warren's love.

"I'm listening," Warren urged. "I have broad shoulders, and maybe it will help to talk about it.

Her voice was barely audible as she began her story. She told him everything. When she finished, he came over beside her, cradling her gently in his arms, as they watched the flickering flames. They sat there until the flames died to flowing embers. Then Janene rose, and without a word climbed the stairs to her rooms.

It was a cold day in mid-January. Snow was falling lightly. Janene stood by the window, rubbing her aching neck muscles. Since her return in late December, things had settled down in a normal routine. She and Warren had worked feverishly on his book, and today, then days ahead of schedule, she had finished typing the last of the manuscript. Tomorrow, Warren would post it to his publisher.

They had developed a warm, satisfying relationship, and strangely enough, there was absolutely no tension between them. At times, when she considered it seriously, she doubted if Warren had ever truly loved her in the real sense. That he cared for her, she didn't doubt, but she had come to believe, over the past weeks, that he was secretly relieved she had not accepted his proposal. He was a lonely man, without family, and in her, he had visualized a sort of security to his old age. She firmly believed he neither needed nor wanted a wife, only companionship. That she had been willing to give, at least temporarily. The ties binding them had grown even stronger. They had even discussed the prospect of her continuing to work for him, but in a less demanding capacity. That way, she would have time to pursue her own writing. Although she had not decided definitely, she was considering the position. It offered countless opportunity for travel, as well as a creative atmosphere in which to work. Few novice writers had the opportunity of learning and growing under the tutelage and direction of an eminently successful writer. Her writing preference leaned toward light romantic and historical fiction. Warren's interest encompassed nonfiction. The techniques of writing good copy remained essentially the same. If only she could be sure that Warren would not make personal demands as well, but she had no guarantee of that. Frankly, she doubted that he would. Still and all, it was a gamble. She didn't want a next time.

The doorbell rang, piercing her thoughts sharply. She ignored it, knowing Sarah Jane, the day maid, or Sam, would take care of it. Vaguely, she wondered where Warren might be. She had been confined in the study-library since early morning. Determined to finish, she'd even taken lunch at her typewriter. She glanced at her watch – five-thirty. She'd have time for a shower and a brief rest before dinner. She turned from the window, and was just putting the cover on the typewriter, when Warren came in.

She glanced up, smiling. "I'm finished, you can post it tomorrow."

"Good," he said, absently, crossing over to stand beside her. As she straightened and turned, he placed both hands on her shoulders, causing her to halt and look at him questioningly.

"Did you hear the doorbell?" She nodded, a sudden feeling of apprehension engulfing her.

"What is it, Warren? Is anything wrong? My family?"

"No, nothing like that," he said, grimly. "There's a man in the living room to see you. He says his name is Vance Reeves."

The color drained from Janene's face, and she swayed dizzily. She was glad Warren's arms were there to steady her. "It's him, isn't it?" he growled. She nodded, knowing at once to whom he referred.

"I don't want to see him, Warren. Please get rid of him," she pleaded, on the verge of tears.

"I can't, I already tried. He said you'd probably refuse to see him. He knew you were here, and said he'd set up camp in the living room if necessary. One way or other, he intended to see you."

"What's he doing here, and how did he find me anyway?"

"I can't answer that," he said.

"No, of course you can't. I'm sorry. But I won't see him. I won't. He hasn't any right to ask that of me. It's been over a year since I last saw him."

"I know, but I think you'd better see him, Janene."

"I can't, is there no other way? What can I do?"

He shook his head, releasing her. "Are you okay?" he asked worriedly.

"Yes. I just don't know what to do."

"You'll think of something. I'd better get back out there. I wouldn't put it past him to storm in here. Remember, if you need me for anything at all, I'm here, and I'll stay with you until you tell me to leave, no matter what the scoundrel says. Okay?" His hand was on the doorknob, but he had paused to smile at her encouragingly. "Oh, Janene, if you'd like some time to compose yourself, or freshen up, I'll stall him. In that closet, there's a hidden stairway that opens directly into my room. Use it and dash upstairs to your rooms if you like." With that, he opened the door, exited, and closed it behind him.

Janene stood for several minutes. Her legs had a rubbery quality that threatened they would desert her if she moved. Her stomach churned, and her hands twisted nervously. Slowly, she walked to the closet door Warren had indicated. She had not known of the secret staircase before. She climbed it with great effort, emerging into an enormous bedroom. Oblivious to her surroundings, she hastily crossed the room, stealthily opening the door leading to the hall. She could hear the faint murmur of male voices as she neared the central corridor. She raced to her own room, realizing as she closed the door behind her, that she was holding her breath.

She walked to her balcony, and stepped outside. It was cold, and the crisp air revived her rapidly. She walked back into the room, heading for the dressing room. Splashing her face vigorously with cold water, and patting it dry, she critically surveyed her image. She was pale, but otherwise appeared normal. She applied fresh make-up, and brushed her hair. She discarded the idea of changing, deciding the turquoise pants suit she wore would do.

As she opened the door to the corridor, panic set in. Squaring her shoulders, and taking a few deep breaths, she shrugged it off. As she neared the central corridor, she hesitated, but then determinedly continued down the stairs. She was quaking inside, and would have been surprised at the poised, composed outward image she presented.

# Chapter 17

As she stepped down into the living room, both men turned toward her. It was a jolt seeing Vance again, but she prayed it would not show. He was thinner than she remembered. His face more lined, and he looked tired. She crossed the room unhurriedly, extending her hand to Vance. He took it, squeezing it intimately. She withdrew it quickly.

"Good evening, Vance. So good to see you again." She smiled sweetly, surprised to find her voice steady. "How about fixing us a drink, Warren, dear?" she said, moving nearer to him. He followed her cue beautifully, saying, "The usual, darling?" She nodded. "And what will you have, Mr. Reeves?"

"Scotch on the rocks," Vance replied, cryptically. Janene sensed his eyes upon her, and she risked a brief glance. A deep puzzled frown creased his forehead, but his eyes, as they met hers momentarily, told her nothing. A cynical smile began to form on his lips as she looked away from his gaze.

"It's more comfortable in the den, Vance," she said coolly, following Warren into that room. "Please sit down," she invited, choosing one of the leather chairs for herself.

Vance lowered his length onto the sofa. She found his arrogant ease irritating. Warren brought their drinks. She murmured her thanks, flashing him a sweet smile as he handed her the drink. He winked rakishly before returning to the bar for his own glass. He sat down casually on the arm of Janene's chair, his arm flung across it's back as if it belonged there naturally.

She lifted the drink to her lips, using her eyelashes to veil her eyes as she looked at Vance. His eyes were on her hand, and she realized he had spotted Warren's ring. The frown deepened on his forehead as he started to raise his eyes.

She relaxed, avoiding his gaze. This was going to be easier than she thought. She chided herself mentally for the malicious pleasure she was getting at seeing Vance's consternation, however mild.

"And what brings you to Seattle Vance?" she asked, coyly glancing in his direction, but not really looking at him.

"I came to see you," he replied, bluntly.

"I can't think whatever for," she retorted honestly.

"You made me a promise some time back," he drawled. "I figured I might like to know why you chose not to keep it."

A shocked gasp caused Janene to choke. Warren patted her back lightly.

"Are you okay?" he asked. At her nod, he moved in front of her, blocking Vance's view on the pretense of re-filling his glass. Janene was grateful for the chance to regain her composure. By the time Warren moved to the bar, she was once again in control.

"When did you leave California?" Vance asked, changing the subject sharply.

"I resigned in August. I'd started writing a book in the late spring, and I decided it required more of my time than my job would allow."

"I see," Vance muttered, caustically.

The telephone shrilled sharply. Warren had to cross to the far side of the room to answer it. It was then that Vance made his move. He arose quickly, and leaning over her chair, whispered.

"Janene, I must talk to you alone. Come with me for a drive. Give Fielding some excuse."

"I don't think we have anything to talk about. Why don't you just go, Vance?"

"Dammit, I don't want to go. Not until you give me some plausible explanation for running out on me," he demanded, grabbing her wrist in a vice-like grip, and forcing her to meet his eyes.

"How dare you? Me, run out on you? That's a laugh," she snapped, her eyes blazing fury as she twisted from his grasp and stood up.

Vance caught her easily about the waist, and turned her toward him. His eyes smoldering, he drew her slowly to him. His touch seemed to brand her with fiery heat. "Let me go," she hissed as she swung her arm wildly hoping to connect with his arrogant face. He caught the arm, deftly twisting it behind her. He would have crushed her to him brutally at that point, had Warren's quiet voice not halted him as he bent his head to seek her lips.

"I believe the lady asked you to leave, Reeves."

Vance released her, but did not immediately remove his arm from about her waist.

"This is my home, Reeves, and I believe you've overstayed your welcome. Now, do leave peacefully, or shall I be forced to throw you out?"

The two men eyed each other warily, poised. Janene felt Vance's arm stiffen as he moved away from her.

She placed a hand on his forearm. "Please, Vance, just go."

"All right, kitten," he drawled, using his pet name for her. "On one condition - that you agree to meet me without the presence of your aging bodyguard."

Warren's face flushed with anger, but he did not move.

"All right, Vance," she murmured.

"Where – when?" he asked, pointedly holding her gaze intently.

"Tomorrow. I'll meet you for lunch at Ivar's Pier 51 at 12:30."

"Fine, I'll be waiting. Don't bother to see me out. I know the way." With a flashing grin, he walked past Warren and out of the room. Seconds later, the front door slammed behind him. Warren had followed Vance's exit as far as the living room.

When he returned, Janene sat in the chair, her head buried in her hands. Warren knelt beside her, placing a gentle hand on her shoulder.

"Oh, Warren," she cried. "I'm so sorry. He had no right to - - -"

"It's all right, Janene. After all, I am an old man in his eyes. Forget it. It doesn't matter."

"Well, it does to me. You are so gentle and kind. He's hateful, despicable, and rude."

"He is a rather arrogant cuss," Warren admitted. "What did he mean about you running out on him?"

"I don't know. I told you why I left California, about the clipping and all."

"Is there any chance someone else could have sent you that clipping, and Mr. Vance Reeves doesn't know anything about it?" Warren asked, thoughtfully.

"I don't see how," Janene answered, considering his question carefully. "No one knew about Vance and me, except his chauffer and housekeeper, and maybe, the doctor. I've never told anyone, except you, not even my parents. He was the only one, except Charles, to know my address. I doubt that Charles would have remembered, as he didn't drive us there, as you know."

"Something doesn't ring true, Janene," Warren commented, reflectively. "The guy's crazy about you, Janene, and he's either confused about losing you, or he's a Goddamn good actor. It's the only logical explanation for his traveling clean across country to find you."

"How do you know that?"

"I asked him. In fact, while you were upstairs, we talked quite freely."

"What about?"

"You, mostly. He asked me where we'd met, and what our relationship was."

"What did you tell him?"

"The truth, up to a point. I told him I'd asked you to marry me. I didn't add that you'd refused."

"What did he have to say?" she asked.

"He said he was in New York when your book came out. He didn't explain how, where, or why. Just that he'd obtained your home address, which led him here."

"He must have contacted my parents, then," Janene exclaimed.

"Could be; does that matter?"

"No, not really; it depends upon how much he told them. They'll just be a little confused, is all."

"Are you going to meet him? You don't have to, you know. We can take the boat and hit the open seas."

"Thanks for the thought, Warren, but I want this over and done with. I've another book to write, you know."

Warren made them another drink, and they sat in comfortable silence until Sarah Jane announced dinner.

Later, as they were having coffee, once again seated in the den, Warren asked, soberly, "Do you still love him, Janene?"

"I don't know. Whether I do or not, I don't intend to find out. I'm not setting myself up for another let down."

"You might be making a mistake," Warren remarked, seriously.

"Hey, whose side are you on?"

"Yours, naturally. But if the guy really loves you, and you love him, well…." He broke off, thoughtfully. "Do you want me to be around tomorrow?"

"No, I'll take the car; then, if I need an escape, I'll have it. I'm not looking forward to my luncheon date much. I just can't understand why he turned up now, after all this time."

"You have no idea what he does, nor what he was involved in that set him up for target practice?"

Janene shook her head. "I was not only blind, I was stupid. I actually know nothing about him. At the time, it didn't seem important. Don't worry, I'll not make that mistake again."

"Have you thought any more about remaining on with me?" Warren asked.

"Yes, but I really haven't decided. I'll let you know in a day or two. I think I'll go to bed, Warren. Good night."

He watched her leave the room with a forlorn, bleak expression. It would have caused Janene grave concern had she seen that look.

# Chapter 18

At exactly twelve-thirty the next day, Janene pulled Warren's shiny, blue Pinto into the Ivar's parking lot. The wind was crispy chilly, and she drew her white mock fur coat more closely around her neck. Her black-heeled calf-boots clicked on the pavement. She did not see him at first, and was debating whether to request a table or not, when she saw his tall, lanky figure move toward her.

She wasn't the only woman in the place watching him. He wore grey slacks, and a grey turtleneck sweater, with a blue and white chest design. His black hair waved in Rock Hudson fashion. She had to admit he was by far the most attractive man she'd even known. Her heart fluttered dangerously at his broad, sensuous smile. She could almost feel the pressure of his lips, tantalizing her own. 'Stop it,' she scolded herself, sharply. 'Keep it light and cool, remember.'

"I was afraid you might not come," he confessed, taking her hand to lead her to his table.

"I usually keep my word," she answered, and immediately wished she'd chosen a different turn of phrase. His grey eyes locked hers in a penetrating gaze, but he said nothing.

They talked generally at first, both avoiding the real reason behind their meeting. They ordered lobster, enjoying it with relish. It was over dessert and coffee that

Vance abruptly plunged into the reason for his wanting to see her.

"Janene, why did you leave California without telling me?"

"I told you that already."

"No, you gave me an excuse for leaving, but why didn't you let me know?"

"Two reasons," she answered. "I didn't know how or where to reach you."

"You could have called The Manor."

"I did, and I talked to Charles. He said you were closing the house indefinitely, and he didn't know where you were, or he wouldn't tell me."

"He didn't know at that time. I was on my way to Greece. I called him later and gave him an address – he was to give it to no one except you. I had him transfer my manor phone number to his phone, so anyone trying to contact The Manor would inevitably reach him. I couldn't expect him to remain at The Manor, as I didn't know how long I'd be gone. He still checked the place, and saw to its upkeep. We have done this sort of thing before when I'm out of the country for extended periods. I presumed he thought you knew that, but, of course, I had neglected to tell you that, hadn't I? I take it you only called The Manor that one time?"

She nodded, replying, "I didn't think there was any use to call again, as no one would be there, and Charles said the phone to The Manor was to be disconnected the following day."

"I see," Vance remarked, thoughtfully. "I guess I

didn't make things very clear to either you or Charles. All I can say is, I'm sorry. I had a lot of things on my mind at that particular time. I felt like I'd known you all my life, and I thoughtlessly left too many things unsaid."

Janene looked at him steadily before saying, softly, "Our trouble was we didn't know enough about each other, I guess."

"Perhaps, but at the time, I knew all that was necessary. That I loved you. I still do," he said, huskily, lifting her hand gently to his lips. She withdrew her hand quickly, avoiding his gaze, to look instead across the water of the Sound.

He lit a cigarette, his eyes watching her.

"You said two reasons," he reminded her. "What was the second?"

"The clipping," she answered, turning to watch his reaction.

"What clipping?" he asked, clearly puzzled. She didn't answer immediately. Fleetingly, doubt that he had sent it crossed her mind. Just as quickly, she shoved the doubt aside. Logically, she knew no one else could have been responsible. She smiled, recalling Warren's words that he must be a damn good actor.

"What clipping are you talking about?" he asked again.

"The one announcing your betrothal."

"My what?" he shouted, then lowered his voice, as several heads turned their direction. Janene lowered her head, sipping the fresh, hot coffee.

"Did you say my betrothal?" he whispered, harshly.

She nodded. "But I've never been engaged, only to you, and I sure as hell didn't announce that to the newspaper. Remember, I wanted to keep you out of that shooting mess."

"I remember," she said, quietly. There was silence, and she could tell from his face that his thoughts were deeply set in the past.

"What did this clipping say?" he asked, finally.

"That's the point. It didn't tell anything. It was just a picture with an overhead caption. The picture was of you with your arm around the shoulders of a stunning blond. Both of you seemed to have eyes only for each other. The caption read, 'Betrothal in the Wind.'" she explained, carefully.

"And that's all. No postmark, return address, note?"

"Nothing. The postmark was blurred. All I could make out was that it was mailed in California."

"Do you still have it?"

"No, I tore it to shreds and threw it away. It was shortly after that I decided I needed a change of scene. I've always wanted to write, so I began a novel. I resigned my job, spent a few months with my parents, met Warren, and went to work for him. I had finished my novel, and I needed a job to tide me over until I found out if my book would sell. He's a successful writer, and the opportunity to work for him gave me valuable experience.

"Do you love him?" Vance asked, hoarsely. Janene didn't answer, and he didn't repeat the question.

"Do you have any idea who sent the clipping to you? Was it a newspaper clipping?"

Janene nodded, then added, "I thought you sent the clipping."

"Did you actually believe I'd take such a cowardly way out?" he asked, grimly.

"Not at first. It seemed out of character, but then I didn't know you all that well, either. As time went on, I realized that since no one else knew of our relationship, it had to be you. I guess I still hoped I was wrong. After all, I didn't leave California until August. Over seven months after we met. By then, I'd accepted the truth."

"But it isn't the truth, kitten," he said, softly, taking her face between his hands, and forcing her to look straight into his eyes. "I did not send you any newspaper clipping. Furthermore, no such clipping ever appeared in any newspaper, of which I'm aware. Can you describe the woman more fully?"

Janene pulled his hands away from her face, but she did not withdraw from his clasp. Her brow pierced in thoughtful concentration, as she tried to recall the photo.

"She was quite tall, reaching just above your shoulder. She was beautiful, in a classic sort of way, rather the Joan Fontaine type. Her hair appeared to be blond, and was probably long. In the picture, it was pinned up on the back of her head, a French roll, I think. She was wearing a long, white fur coat."

"Mona," he guessed, immediately. "It has to be Mona. She's the only woman I can recall having in any picture with me, but I never was, nor do I ever plan to be, engaged to Mona Richards."

She did not ask him who Mona Richards was, but something in her eyes must have prompted him to elaborate.

"Mona and I are old friends. I've escorted her places from time to time, primarily because I admire her father and his work. In fact, I've had the pleasure of working with him on project sites occasionally. Mona is a newspaper photographer. She would have access to newsprint. It wouldn't be too hard to fake a clipping like you received. It's the sort of thing Mona might do. To put it mildly, darling, she's a conniving, scheming bitch. She sharpened her claws on me more than once. She's cast sheep's eyes in my direction for years, but there's never been anything between us. She'd make a man's life sheer unadulterated hell."

"Were you lovers?" Janene asked, then added, "I'm sorry, you don't need to answer that. It's none of my business."

"You're right, it's a dumb question, and none of your business, but I'll answer it anyway. No, we were never lovers. Not that she wouldn't have cooperated. I'm just not that much of a fool."

"Do you know how that sounds?" she asked with a smile.

"Conceited as hell, but it's true."

The waitress appeared to refill their coffee cups, so they both fell silent. Janene became absorbed in watching some gulls fighting over a fish. Vance stirred his coffee absently.

"All right, I can understand why you left California, and accept that, but why didn't you leave a forwarding address?"

"It wasn't necessary. By the time I left California, I'd had time to inform all my friends, etc., of the address change."

"And you didn't' want me to know where you'd gone."

"That never occurred to me. I felt that too much time had elapsed, and I never expected to hear from you again. Remember, I believed you'd probably married by that time! I'd received the clipping in early spring."

"There's one thing about that clipping I still can't figure out. I carried your address and phone number in my head. I never wrote it down anywhere. The only other person that knew it, to my knowledge, was Charles, and he detested Mona, so I know he wouldn't have given it to her. And I damn sure didn't. To my knowledge, she never knew your name. You didn't happen to tell her your name when she called at The Manor while you were there, did you?"

"No, I did not. She asked me a couple of times, but I ignored the question. As far as I know, only your doctor, the nurse, and Charles knew my name."

"It's unlikely any of them would or could have told Mona either. She never knew about the shooting incident."

"There's lots of ways for reporters to uncover stories, you know, Vance."

"Right, but I can't visualize Mona going to all that effort. She, basically, is a very lazy person. I guess it doesn't really matter now, anyway."

He was still holding her left hand, and she was suddenly aware that he was toying with her ring. "This is his ring, isn't it?" he asked. She nodded. "Are you going to marry him?"

"That, Mr. Reeves, is my business," she replied, coolly.

"What about us?" he asked.

"That's over, Vance. We can't turn back the clock."

"We don't have to, all we have to do is pick up where we left off."

"And I don't want to."

"I still love you, kitten. I've never stopped loving you. For a time, circumstances prevented me from coming to you, then, when I did, I couldn't find you. I've been half-crazy the last few months, alternately longing for you, and cursing the day I met you. You're in my blood, that hasn't changed — not since the moment I first saw you sitting on that suitcase, looking lost and dejected. Can you tell me, in all honesty, that you don't love me?" When she didn't answer, he grinned, boyishly triumphant. "I thought not. Why didn't you tell your parents about me?"

"At first, it seemed best not to, and then it was just easier and pointless."

"Didn't you ever tell anyone?"

"Yes, I told Warren."

"So that's why he recognized me so quickly."

"No, he simply guessed. I never mentioned you by name. By the way, Vance, what did you tell my parents?" she asked, curiously.

"Not much. I introduced myself, and pretended I was there to interview you for publicity on your novel. I was pretty good. I took notes like a real pro. I reported I'd heard a rumor of an engagement. They said no, so I knew you hadn't told them about me. Your mother gave me Fielding's address, and here I am."

Janene glanced at her watch; it was nearing three. "I really must go, Vance," she said, starting to rise. His grasp on her hand retained her.

"Not just yet, please, kitten."

Reluctantly, she settled back in the seat.

"When can I see you again?" he asked, softly. "Doesn't the fact I still love you mean anything to you at all? Why won't you let me make this last year up to you? We could be happy; I know it. I realize that unintentionally I've hurt you badly, but it hasn't exactly been heaven on earth for me, either. You haven't any idea how my mind has tortured me these past months, as I tried to figure out why you ran out on me. The only person I dared discuss it with was Charles, and he was damn little help. Hell, he didn't even tell me you'd called. I suppose he forgot about it, but if he had, it would have given me some hope. As it was, I thought that once you'd left The Manor, you erased me from heart and mind. After I came back to the States, in late August, I tried my best to exorcise you. I couldn't, and when I saw your book, I knew then I'd never rest until I found you again."

"Vance, listen to me, please. Things are different now. Besides there being too much water under the bridge, I have my career to consider. I've been commissioned to write a second novel," she lied, blatantly. "It's what I want to do. I don't have time for marriage. I'm not even sure I want it."

"You mean, you don't want marriage to me," he groaned, hoarsely. "Hell, you won't even admit you still love me, will you?"

"I'm sorry, Vance."

"I won't let you go without a fight, you know that, don't you? Either tell me honestly you don't feel anything for me, that you don't love me, and never want to see me again, otherwise, I'll pester and plague you until you come into my arms, begging for mercy."

"I don't want to hear anymore of this," she said. "Goodbye, Vance." She slid from her chair quickly, and hurried across the restaurant toward the exit. She was over half way when he caught up with her. An iron grasp on her forearm spun her around to face him, slamming her hard against his muscular chest.

"Where do you think you're going" he hissed, loudly.

"I'm leaving. I told you that."

"Not like that, you're not," he said, pinning her arms against his chest, as his own encircled her, and drew her even closer. Before she had time to assess his intentions, his lips smothered hers in a violently brutal kiss. Her mouth opened to speak, his tongue found its target and met hers, evoking the response it sought. Resistance melted as he re-kindled the passionate flame she'd buried. Cheering and clapping parted them. Janene was blushing heatedly, and she prayed the floor would open and swallow her up. Vance, on the other hand, was not the least embarrassed. He raised his hand to signal the crowd to silence as he said clearly to her, "Now perhaps you'll behave?" Then to the silent crowd, he apologized. "Sorry folks, just a little misunderstanding. I think she realizes who's the boss now," and with his arm still about her waist, he winked at the crowd, rakishly. Immediately, the clapping and cheering began again. As he passed the cash register, he tossed a fifty dollar bill at the teller, ushering Janene outside with him.

Once in the open air, she turned on him, angrily. "I'll never forgive you for that despicable display."

"Oh, yes you will, kitten," he said, arrogantly unconcerned. She jerked from his encircling arm only to have her wrist caught in his unbreakable grip.

At her car, he released her. She was still fuming. He stood watching her, silently, as she unlocked the car door and slid beneath the wheel. "Aren't you going to offer me a lift?" he grinned, teasingly.

"No," she snapped.

"Temper, temper," he taunted, catching the edge of the door as she tried to slam it in his face. Leaning toward her, he whispered, "At least I have my answer, kitten. Whether you're willing to admit or accept it, you still love me." He brushed her lips in a gentle caress as she turned to deliver a scathing retort. Then he closed the car door, waved jauntily, and walked away, hands in his pockets. Somehow, she knew he was whistling, and furiously, she pulled the car onto the street, the tires screeching.

# Chapter 19

By the time Janene reached her destination, she had calmed down. Still, she was vastly relieved that Warren was not about. She was physically and emotionally exhausted. She went straight to her rooms, took a lengthy shower, and lay down upon her bed. She had only intended to rest for a short time, but she soon fell soundly asleep.

Janene was surprised to find it morning. It took her a moment to realize that her telephone was buzzing. The huge house had telephones in nearly all rooms, but rather than having phones ringing all over the house, Warren had installed only two which recorded outside rings. Whoever answered must then buzz one of the other rooms, if another person was required to answer the phone. This prevented Warren from having to interrupt his writing.

"Yes," Janene answered.

"Call for you, Miss Janene. Do you wish to receive it?" Sarah Jane's gentle voice demanded.

"Who is it?"

"I don't know, Miss. The man would not leave his name."

"All right, Sarah Jane, I'll take it."

There was a brief click, and Janene answered once more. "Good morning, kitten," drawled the deep male voice, smoothly. "Are you still mad at me?"

"Furious," she replied, but her lips twitched in a smile.

"Spend the day with me?" the voice asked.

"No," came the quick reply.

"Why not? It's Sunday; we'll have breakfast, and tour the city. This is my first trip to Seattle, you know?"

"No, I didn't know, and the answer is still no."

"Coward," he challenged, and she realized he was right. There was no reason why she couldn't spend the day with Vance. Warren was gone for the weekend. She really had nothing else to do. Even though she knew it was folly, she wanted to spend the day with Vance. Could she do that and keep her heart intact? She shrugged undecidedly.

Taking her silence as acquiescence, Vance added lightly, "I've rented a car, so I'll pick you up in forty minutes. I love you, kitten." The line went dead.

She stared at it for a moment before replacing the receiver and bounding out of bed. She had an idea she was going to regret this day, but at the moment she felt too good to care. She giggled remembering how mad and embarrassed she was at Vance's kissing her in front of all those people. She was forced, begrudgingly, to admire his insolence, but then she doubted that seldom, if ever, was that aura of self-assurance even dented. After all, his good looks, coupled with a lion's strength and arrogance, aided by wealth, would always land him at the top of the heap.

Janene had no idea just what plans Vance had for the day. It was warmer than yesterday, but still very crisp. A light drizzle fell steadily. She chose to wear black work slacks, and calf boots, and a red cowl-necked sweater. She secured a black patent rain hat to her head, adding a slicker coat. As an after-thought, she decided to carry an umbrella. A Seattle drizzle could become a torrential downpour at any time.

She was coming down the central stairs when the doorbell rang. She called to Sarah Jane that she would get it, and opened the door. She hardly recognized him in his hat and topcoat, for she had never seen him in a hat before.

They breakfasted at an International Pancake House, then spent some time at the Seattle Center. They explored the shops on Pike Street, had luncheon at an Irish Pub-style restaurant in the vicinity. All in all, it had been an enjoyable day. Vance had kept their relationship lightly impersonal, almost as if he sensed she did not need another assault on her emotions now.

It was after nine when he drove her back to Warren's estate. He kissed her lightly, barely brushing his lips along hers, and left.

Happily content, she let herself in the front door, and started toward her room.

"Is that you, Janene?" Warren called, coming from the den with a drink in his hand. "Would you care for something?"

"No, thanks, but I'll join you for a few minutes, if you have a fire going. Brrr, but it's cold outside," she added, removing her coat to stand toasting in front of the fireplace.

Warren was seated in a nearby chair, idly watching

her. She was unaware of her attractiveness. Her eyes held a sparkling luster, her cheeks rosy from the out-of-doors, her slim figure sleek and chic in her outfit. The loosely fitting sweater nevertheless hinted that firm well-rounded breasts were hidden subtly beneath. Her ash-blonde hair, longer than she usually wore it, was secured by a wide red band. Warren indolently appraised her looks, but it was not her beauty that held his gaze. For the first time since meeting her, she looked vibrant and fully alive. Always alert, and sensitive to the feelings of others, she had remained coolly aloof and remote. He quickly dropped his eyes as she turned toward him. He did not want to reveal his own sorrow. Whether she admitted it or not, he could visibly see the change Vance Reeves' sudden appearance had wrought. Without the slightest doubt, he knew she was lost to him forever.

"Did you post your manuscript?" she asked, earnestly. He nodded.

"Did you spend the day with Reeves?" he asked, curiously.

She nodded her assent but did not elaborate, so he added casually, "I take it your luncheon date was a success, then."

She chuckled, throatily. "Not exactly. I walked out on him, blazing mad." He looked at her questioningly. She hesitated briefly, then told him of the spectacle Vance had created in Ivar's. "I can laugh about it now, but I was thoroughly embarrassed, and boiling mad, at the time," she explained.

"He's the brash one, all right," was Warren's caustic comment. "I take it you kissed and made up today."

"Actually, no," she answered, and briefly told him about her day. She was unaware of the warmth and tenderness her eyes revealed as she talked of Vance. Warren fixed himself another drink while she talked. his own feelings raw as he watched and listened to her. He found himself hating Reeves, silently, but listened, feigning interest. Her question startled him.

"How was your weekend, Warren?" Her smile was warm and genuine, piercing the pit of his stomach like a sharp knife.

"Fine," he lied, not wanting her to know how lonely and lost he'd really felt, torn between the desire to follow her to Ivar's, and forcefully carry her away from Reeves, and the knowledge that she neither wanted, nor would have accepted, such an action from him.

She turned once more to face the fire as silence fell heavily upon the room, broken only by the crackling embers as they blazed away.

Some minutes later, Warren broke the silence with his question. "So, what comes next?"

Receiving no answer, he continued. "I've decided to leave for Egypt right after the first of the month. What are your plans?"

"I'm afraid I haven't made any yet," she replied, honestly.

"I see. Oh, well, I'll make reservations for two. One can always be cancelled later, if you decide not to go."

"That's fine, Warren," she answered vaguely.

"What does Reeves do for a living?" he asked, mildly curious.

A bewildered stare met his intent eyes. Then, she laughed nervously. "I don't really know. The subject just never came up."

"So, you still don't know if he's a rich playboy, or a henchman for the Mafia," he commented with a tinge of sarcasm.

"No, I guess I don't," she admitted, reluctantly.

"Really, Janene, I think you owe it to yourself to find out what the man does before you become any more involved with him."

"I'm not becoming involved with him," she snapped quickly, too quickly Warren noted, but he said no more.

Presently, Janene announced she was going to her rooms. He watched her retreating figure, the lines on his face deepening. He fixed himself another drink – a double this time, and sat staring into space.

In her room, Janene's troubled thoughts refused to rest. She knew Warren had not meant to upset her. However, his question about Vance's occupation had brought home to her, sternly, the realization that she still knew next to nothing about Mr. Vance Reeves. Deciding to remedy that factor on their next encounter, she was brought face to face with another realization. She not only expected to see Vance again, she was looking forward to it. 'You're a complete fool,' she chided her reflection in the mirror. 'Why don't you just take off to Egypt with Warren, and put Mr. Vance Reeves out of your life for good?' Even as she put the thought into words, she doubted her strength to resist that blatant Reeves charm.

# Chapter 20

Janene slept fitfully. Her dreams filled with a mocking Vance Reeves, sinister Mafia strong boys, and Egyptian pyramids. She awoke head-achy and irritable. She breakfasted alone in her small kitchenette. Afterwards, she showered, dressed, did some laundry, and tidied her bedroom. She attempted to write some letters, but found she was too restless. She missed the demanding work Warren's writing had provided. She had to make a decision soon. Her present state of mind would accomplish nothing. The buzz of the phone caused her to jump.

"Call for you, Miss Janene," Sarah Jane's voice announced.

"All right, Sarah Jane." There was the customary click, and then she heard Vance's voice asking, "Lunch with me, kitten?"

"All right," she answered, wearily.

"My, such enthusiasm overwhelms me," he teased. "Is anything wrong?"

"No," came her clipped reply.

"I'll pick you up in 30 minutes."

She turned from the phone unenthusiastically. She re-applied lipstick, flipped a brush through her hair, and secured it with a headband. Though it was overcast outside, it was not raining. She felt depressed, her mood matching the weather, and she wished she'd refused

Vance's invitation. She grabbed the black slicker, hat, and her purse, and went slowly downstairs. At the front door, she put on her coat and hat, and let herself outside. She was walking aimlessly down the circular driveway toward the street below, when Vance's car drew along side. He reached across the seat to open the door. She climbed in and settled herself back against the cushions.

"Good morning, kitten," he said softly, as he urged the car forward. She smiled wanly, but did not return the greeting.

He maneuvered the car skillfully through city traffic, and onto the freeway, heading north.

"Where are we going?" she asked.

"Nowhere and anywhere," was his answer. They rode along in silence for a number of miles.

"Why so quiet?" he asked abruptly.

"Just nothing to say, I guess," she replied. He chuckled, but made no more attempts at conversation. Some miles away from the city, he guided the car off the freeway. He pulled into a service station. After purchasing gasoline, he returned to the car. A short time later, he parked in front of a nondescript roadside restaurant, somewhere South of Everett. Afterwards, neither could have remembered the name of the place, nor what they'd eaten.

"What's wrong, kitten?" Vance asked, with worried concern, once they had been seated, and placed their order. Janene had endured his shrewd scrutiny in silence, fully aware that he was puzzled by her behavior. She, too, was puzzled. She felt uncomfortable, gauche, and on the verge of tears. Her head ached, her mouth was dry, and she knew she was rotten company. She lacked the will to do anything toward shrugging off the mounting depression. What's more, she didn't know why she was so miserable.

"I've a headache," she replied, woefully. "I'm sure rotten company, perhaps it would be best if you just took me home."

He arose and disappeared toward the entrance. When he returned, he carried a container of headache tablets.

"Here, take a couple of these, then if you aren't feeling better, I'll take you back. You don't suppose you're coming down with something, do you?"

She shook her head negatively as she swallowed two of the tablets. By the time he'd finished lunch, she was in somewhat better spirits. She ate very little, but the hot coffee helped revive her to some extent. He had chattered continuously through lunch, paying no attention to her lack of response. She even managed a weak smile or two at his quips about various people who wandered in and out of the restaurant. It occurred to her, as she listened absently to his chatter, that he talked nothing of himself.

"Do you have any brothers or sisters?" she asked abruptly.

He looked at her curiously before replying, "No, I haven't any family, except for a Great Aunt who resides in Sidney."

"Sidney, Australia?" she asked.

"Yes, I'm an Aussie. At least, I was born there. My

parents were killed in a plane crash, while I was still in college, along with my younger sister."

"I'm sorry," she said quietly.

"No matter, it was a long time ago. I've been pretty much of a loner ever since."

"Where did you go to school?"

"U.C.L.A.," he answered, reflectively. She thought he was going to leave it there, but she hesitated to ask further questions. She had felt the reticence in him when the conversation had turned toward his personal life and background. This confused her, and she vaguely wondered if he was hiding something. She glanced at him overtly. He had a faraway expression of deep concentration, and did not see her look. She dropped her eyes to her hands, encircling the coffee mug on the table in front of her. It was several minutes before he spoke. His voice was low, almost as if he were talking to himself.

"I've always thought someday I'd go back to Australia to live, but I haven't made it yet. My mother was born near Sidney. She and my father met at the University there. She was a student, and he a visiting professor. From what I've been told, theirs was a whirlwind courtship, and they were married only a short time later. My father's great love was to study ancient civilizations. I guess that's what inspired me to become an archeologist. Anyway, I went to U.C.L.A., got my degree, and headed for parts unknown," he paused, and flashed her a quick smile. "Feeling better?" he asked solicitously.

"Yes, I am," she said. "Please tell me some more about yourself," she urged.

"Well, there's not a great lot to tell," he continued, relaxing visibly. "After college, I worked for a while at various digs in South America and Mexico. It was on one of these that I met Frank Richards. He's one of the top archeologists of today. He persuaded me to join an expedition he was organizing in Peru. I did. The expedition took two years, and was not highly successful. My grandparents lived at Vance Manor, so I returned to the states. I found my grandmother had died, and my grandfather in extremely ill health, so I stayed. After he died, I inherited the Manor. I took over my grandfather's horse racing enterprises, but found it wasn't my bag, and after a couple of years, sold the entire set-up. I was at loose ends and couldn't seem to find anywhere to go with my life. My grandfather was an extremely wealthy man. As his only heir, I inherited everything. Selling the racing stock and stables only increased that wealth."

"Go on," she urged when he paused again.

"Are you sure I'm not boring the hell out of you?" he asked as the waitress refilled their coffee mugs.

"No, I'm really interested. My writer's curiosity is hardly satisfied. Please continue."

"As I said, I was at loose ends, so I tried the jet-set trip. It bored me. They were all so phony and useless. After a few months, I'd decided that was not my kind of life. I wanted to continue my archeological work, but I couldn't seem to find a way to get started. About this time, I met Mona Richards. Frank had never mentioned a daughter, and at first I didn't realize he was her father. Anyway, through her I learned Frank was organizing an expedition into Greece. I went to see him. The expedition couldn't get off the ground for lack of financing, so I agreed to back the project, providing I could go along. Frank was more than agreeable. I was gone nearly three years. In fact, I'd only been back in the States a few months when we met." He fell silent at this point, lit a cigarette, and inhaled deeply.

She studied him steadily, her brow somewhat furrowed.

"There you have it," he quipped. "My life in a nutshell. It ended after I met you," he added huskily. "Why the puzzled look?"

"I don't know," she said hesitantly. "I was trying to fit that shooting incident into that story, I guess."

"What did you think, that I was some sort of gangster?"

"The thought crossed my mind," she answered truthfully.

"Fool, it was nothing so sinister, I guarantee." Seeing this did not satisfy her curiosity, he explained.

"During the Greek expedition, Frank took ill and was forced to return to the States. I was left in charge. The dig was highly successful, as we located the ruins of an ancient city, and uncovered a number of valuable artifacts. I received word, a few months before the expedition was to close, that Frank was dying. Because the expedition was Frank's baby, he wanted to see me to work out some final details. Since work at the site was nearly finished anyway, I put another man in charge, and returned to the States. To make a long story short, some valuable artifacts were stolen from the site. The Greek government was up in arms. Things got pretty hairy for awhile. Some kook in Los Angeles decided to avenge the Greek government by taking a pot-shot at me. The police uncovered this shortly after the shooting. The man insisted he was representing the Greek government, and had papers to back up his claim. The F.B.I. became involved, and the whole thing had the makings of a very messy international incident. I was put under surveillance, ordered to keep the lid on, and to limit, my personal contacts until the thing was cleared. I was warned that anyone close to me might be in danger. That's why I sent you away so suddenly. It was later necessary for me to return to Greece. I left in February and returned in August. February was the last time I saw Mona Richards. We had a blazing row. I told her to get off my back, and out of my life, for good. With Frank Richards no longer alive, I saw no reason why I should put up with her. It's this row, I feel that led her to send you that clipping. How she accomplished it, or what she hoped to gain, I've no idea. I'll probably never prove it, but I'm convinced she had a hand in it somehow."

"She must love you very much," Janene said softly.

"Mona, love me? That's a laugh. Want me, maybe, but love? Never. Mona has never loved anyone but herself. The only reason she bothered with me at all is for my money, and possibly because I was besotted by her genteel looks. No, kitten, Mona Richards does not love me, of that I'm positive."

# Chapter 21

"Shall we go?" she said.

A few minutes later they were cruising down the freeway, heading back toward the city. Neither had spoken since leaving the restaurant, but it was not a strained, uncomfortable silence.

Still, some miles from the city, Vance eased the car into a rest stop area. It was barren and deserted, and Janene vaguely wondered why he was stopped here.

It wasn't long before she found out. He switched off the ignition, and turned toward her.

"Come here, kitten," he coaxed.

She sat rigidly on her own side of the car. Ignoring her, he slid toward her, his arm sliding along the seat behind her, his hand resting lightly on her shoulder. With his free hand, he turned her face toward him. Experimentally, his lips sought hers, expertly searching to evoke her response. Heeding the treacherous warnings of her body, she jerked away from him.

"Don't you think we've had enough of this nonsense? You want me just as much as I want you, and you know it." Still, Janene said nothing.

"Do you know how hard it is for me not to sweep you into my arms the moment I see you? Kiss away your hurt and doubts and make violent love to you? What the hell do you want from me – blood?" he shouted hoarsely.

"I don't want anything," she said calmly.

"Dammit, Janene, I love you. I never said that to any woman. What's more, I want you to be my wife, the mother of my children. Why do you keep pushing me away?" his voice was scarcely a whisper. He drew her rigid body into his arms, his lips seeking hers, his fingertips caressing her throat and cheek. His mouth left hers to plant a trail of fiery kisses along her jawline, her eye lids, and coming to rest in the pulsating hollow of her throat, then captured her lips passionately. She tried in vain to remain passive, but unwillingly, her arms stole about his neck, and she opened her mouth beneath the increasing pressure of his kiss. Once his lips had waked the response they sought, his arms relaxed their hold slightly. When he released her lips, she sat trembling, her head against his chest.

"When will you marry me?" he whispered tenderly. She could hear the pounding of his heart, feel his warm labored breathing against her hair. Slowly, she straightened in the seat. He moved away from her to slide under the wheel. He lit a cigarette as he struggled with his own control.

"You haven't answered my question?" he asked huskily. "Let's get married right away. We can be in Reno in a few hours. What do you say?"

Janene breathed deeply, and when she spoke, her voice was steady and clear.

"I'm not going to marry you, Vance."

"But why? You surely can't deny you love me."

"I told you yesterday why I didn't want to get married."

"Hell, I know what you said, but what about how you feel? Janene, you're a warm, passionate woman. You were meant to be loved, to have a husband and children. I love you so much. I want to be that man, I want to father those children."

"Don't, Vance, please," she whimpered.

"Are you denying that you love me? That you responded to my kisses as warmly and passionately as they were given?" he asked, his voice harsh with suppressed emotion.

"I'm denying nothing. But any man with your expertise could wake the response he wanted from any woman," she replied.

"I see," was the dry answer. "So the only reason you respond to me is that I'm such an expert. You're a damned liar. You love me, and you enjoy being in my arms. You always have, and you still do. Do you doubt that I love you? Tell me how to prove it to you, and I will."

"I know you love me," she said softly. "I also know I love you, but I still will not marry you." He studied her overtly.

"Are you suggesting we just live together? No commitments? Just live together. All right, if that's the way you want it."

"No, Vance, I'm not suggesting that, either. I don't want the hurt and pain that goes along with caring too much for someone."

"But that doesn't make sense. What are you afraid of?"

"Afraid? Yes, I'm afraid. Afraid I'll care too much, then lose it."

"Darling," he said softly. "There's always a risk. If you love somebody, they probably will hurt you from time to time, but that's part of loving, part of life."

"I know that, Vance, but I'm not willing to take that risk. We came from entirely different worlds. I'm an unsophisticated farm girl. You're a man of the world. I can't and won't cope with that."

He sat in rigid silence for some time, then started the car and pulled onto the freeway.

"Nothing I do or say will change your mind. Is that right?" he said finally, his voice betraying defeat. Janene didn't answer, she felt an overwhelming desire to cradle and comfort him, but she suppressed it determinedly. She felt no joy in his pain, but she couldn't bring herself to risk being hurt again. Even his declarations of undying love, and her own logical conclusion that he'd do anything to keep her from being hurt didn't release the fear she harbored inside.

"All right, Janene. You win. I'll be leaving later tonight, as soon as I can get a plane out. I won't bother you again. Another man I could fight, but this fear of life, it's trials and tribulations, I not only can't fight, I can't understand. If you should ever change your mind, call me at the Manor."

"I won't."

"No, I'm sure you won't. I feel sorry for you,

kitten. Life's going to treat you very cruelly, for unless you care and give freely of yourself, nothing will ever have meaning. The worst part of all is I know that somehow I'm responsible for the way you feel. There was a time when you weren't afraid of marrying me, and you weren't afraid of life. Somehow I destroyed that, and now even my love for you drives you further from me. I'm sorry, kitten. I'm sorry we ever met," he said, brokenly, not attempting to stop the tears of wretchedness that ran from his cheeks as he stopped the car in the Fielding driveway. As she fled from the car, he caught her arm, gently whispering, "Forgive me, kitten."

At the front door, Janene fumbled for her key. She glanced back at the car. Vance was slumped dejectedly across the wheel. Her heart jerked, and it took all her will to leave him and go inside. She ran swiftly up the stairs, and flopped face down on the bed, her body torn by racking sobs. Sometime later, she crawled into bed, fully clothed, exhausted.

The next day, she awakened listless and depressed. She didn't bother with breakfast, and she didn't dress. She wandered about the three rooms in a daze, staring vacantly into space. All she could see was Vance's despairing face, and his broken body slumped over the steering wheel of the car. She stayed in her room all day. Warren came up a couple of times, but she would not see him. It was the same the next day, and the following. Finally, the end of the third day, Warren kicked open the sitting room door, and came in.

"What in the hell did Reeves do to you?" he

growled, gruffly scooping her up in his arms, and carrying her downstairs to the den, where a warm fire blazed.

He yelled for Sarah Jane, and ordered beef broth and Jello to be brought immediately into the den. Holding the spoon, he fed her, forcing her to eat and drink every mouthful.

"Now, what's the meaning of this?" he asked harshly, when they had finished. "You look like the wreck of Hesperides. How long have you been wearing those clothes?"

"Since Tuesday, I guess."

"My God, woman, today's Friday - haven't you eaten or slept?"

"I don't know," she answered.

"Okay, you don't know. Fine. But I'm going to take you upstairs. You are going to get out of those clothes, and take a nice, hot shower, and put on a robe. Then, young lady, we're going to have a long talk. I mean it," he said when she eyed him vacantly. "Either you do as I say, or I will personally undress, bathe and re-dress you myself. Do you understand?"

Janene nodded meekly. Leaning weakly on his arm, she walked slowly upstairs with him. Later, feeling more like herself, she emerged from the dressing room, freshly scrubbed, and wearing a full length blue woolen robe.

# Chapter 22

Warren smiled his approval, and escorted her back downstairs to the den. Sarah Jane appeared almost immediately with a steaming pot of hot tea. As she sipped the hot liquid, Warren began his questioning with, "Where's Reeves staying?"

"He's gone."

"What do you mean, gone?"

"I sent him away. He's probably in California," she answered, in a monotone.

"Why did you send him away?"

"Because I didn't want to marry him."

"Why, don't you love him?"

"Yes."

"Then why did you send him away?"

"I don't know."

"Do you want him to come back?"

"No," she said, her eyes wild with panic.

"Did he want to leave?"

"No."

"But you told him to leave."

"Yes."

"Was he agreeable to that?"

"Not at first."

"You convinced him?"

"Yes."
"What did you tell him?"
"That I wouldn't marry him."
"Did you tell him you loved him?"
"Yes."
"But you said you wouldn't marry him?"
"Yes."
"Why did you tell him that?"
"I don't know."
"Do you want to marry him now?"
"No," again the frightened, wild look crossed her face.
"Why are you afraid?"
"I don't know."
"Are you afraid of me?"
"No."
"Are you afraid of Vance?"
"No."
"Did you hurt him?"
"Yes."
"How?"
"I don't know."

Janene had not noticed, but Warren had turned on his recording tape as they talked. His voice was soothingly calm, but his face was lined with worry. He decided to try again.

"Janene, did Vance harm you?"
"No."
"Did you harm Vance?"
"No."

"But you hurt him?"
"Yes."
"How do you know you hurt him?"
"He cried."
"Did this bother you?"
"Yes."
"Did you comfort him?"
"No."
"Why not?"
"I don't know."
"Did you want to comfort him?"
"Yes."
"Then why didn't you?"
"I don't know."
"Do you want to know if he's all right?"
"Yes."
"Shall we call him?"

"No," again the frightened response, but otherwise, she displayed absolutely no emotion. Her eyes were glassy and dazed. He watched her thoughtfully. She sat drinking her tea like a zombie. She would answer if he spoke to her, but offered nothing herself.

After about an hour, he took her back to her rooms. She crawled in bed, and he tucked her in as he might have a child, touching his lips gently to her forehead. Before he'd reached the door of the room, she was asleep.

Downstairs again, he retrieved the tape and went into the study. He replayed the tape twice, listening intently. He switched it off, and sat in thoughtful concentration for several minutes. Then, decisively, he picked up the phone and dialed. He talked briefly, hung up, and dialed again. The second conversation was even shorter. Then he replaced the receiver, thought for a moment, and dialed a third time. This time, he waited, impatiently tapping his fingers on the desk, for the call to go through. The conversation was extensive this time, and he had just replaced the receiver when Sarah Jane rapped, opening the door to allow a tall, lanky, grey-haired man to enter.

"Good evening, Max," Warren greeted. "Thanks for coming."

For some time, the two men talked earnestly. Then, Warren re-played the tape he'd made of his conversation with Janene.

"Well, Max, what do you think?" Warren asked.

"As you know, I can't make a diagnosis without first seeing the patient. But, based on what you've told me, and upon that tape, I'd say she's extremely disturbed. What you described bears out the idea of extreme depression. Have you any idea why she has become so depressed?"

"No, that's what's so puzzling," Warren said, with considerable agitation. "Monday evening she was fine. To my knowledge, she's received no distressing news. She has been working hard, but not that hard."

"Depression is a funny thing," Max said, "but usually some shock or tragedy triggers it, but it can be real or imagined."

What should I do?" Warren asked.

"Give it a few days. She may pull herself out. If not, bring her to my office, and we'll run some clinical tests, etc., and see what we come up with."

Warren escorted Max out, then hurried upstairs, first checking in on a sleeping Janene before going to his own quarters. There, he showered and shaved, packing a small valise.

Half an hour later, he was downstairs, talking earnestly with Sarah Jane. Then, carrying the valise, he left the house.

The next evening, tired and drawn, Warren returned. Janene was still in her room, and Sarah Jane informed him she had not been downstairs all day.

Wearily, he ran a hand through his hair, and trudged heavily upstairs. Janene was sleeping again, or still. He wasn't sure which. Quietly, he left her, went to his own room and showered. Freshly attired, he picked up the phone near his bed and dialed.

"Max," he said, when the voice answered. "Can you come over right away?"

He went downstairs to the den, fixed himself a drink, and sat down.

When Max arrived, Warren explained where he'd been all day, and what he'd learned. Then he quickly outlined a plan, and waited for his friend's reaction.

"It's risky, to say the least, Warren," Max stated thoughtfully. "On the other hand, if you two are right, then it just might work. If Janene has convinced herself that she's incapable of expressing normal human emotions, then her rejection of this guy's love offers her the proof. If he was as broken and miserable as he told you, then her failure to meet his need for her reassurance and love increased her feeling of failure within herself. As you say, he blames himself. Now, she thinks she's destroyed him, so she's blaming herself, and must then be destroyed. Do you understand?"

"I think so. She was fine, and could rationalize her reasons and actions as long as he remained strong and arrogant. But seeing him broken by her rejection was too much for her to accept. Right?"

"That's about it. Do you believe this guy?"

"Yes, I do. He's rather in bad shape himself. What do you mean, there's a risk, Max?"

"Well, in any type of mental or emotional illness, there's a chance further shock might only increase the problem. She could be driven into an even greater depression. In this case, it's hard to say. The young lady sounds like a very strong, stable person. I think given time, she'd probably bring herself around. But you realize that I've never seen the patient."

"Would you see her now?" Warren suggested.

"Fine."

"Give me a few minutes, and I'll see if I can arrange it."

Warren hurried from the room. Janene awakened as he entered, and he was pleased to see her attempt a smile. He asked her to join him for dinner. At first, she seemed on the verge of refusing, but instead, she nodded.

She got up from the bed, and entered the dressing room. She was not long. She had put on the blue robe, applied a bit of lipstick, and brushed her hair.

"You look fine," he complemented, and escorted

her downstairs. He spoke briefly with Sarah Jane in the dining room before escorting Janene into the den.

Max Jacobs arose as they entered.

Warren came forward with an outstretched hand. "Max, this is good of you drop by. Janene, my good friend, Max Jacobs. Max, this is Janene, my secretary, researcher, and co-worker."

"Hello, Janene," Max said.

"How do you do, Mr. Jacobs," she smiled, with a firm clasp.

"Call me Max," he urged.

"All right, Max, please excuse my state of dress. I was not expecting visitors," Janene offered shyly.

"You look fine, Janene."

She sat down easily on the sofa, with Warren taking a seat beside her.

"I understand you've been helping Warren with his latest book," Max commented, pulling Janene into conversation.

"Yes, I have. It's been a wonderful experience, and besides, I enjoy working with Warren, he's such a dear."

"What are you plans now?" he asked gently.

A look of faint bewilderment crossed her face, and then she smiled. "I'm afraid I haven't made any decisions yet. Warren has asked me to go on working for him, but I'm not really sure."

"What do you want to do with your life?"

She was thoughtful for a moment, then said confidently, "I want to write, of course, travel, meet people, see things, you know," she finished vaguely.

"Don't you plan to get married?" Max asked, carefully watching her reaction. Warren, too, was watching Janene closely, for he knew Max was carefully working Janene to a point of admitting what was disturbing her.

"No," she replied, without hesitation.

"Why ever not?" Max said. "I thought all women entertained thoughts of marriage."

"Well, I don't," she replied firmly.

"Why?"

"I just don't think it's necessary. Not for me, anyway."

"What about children?"

"What about them? I like children, as long as they belong to someone else," she smiled, adding, "I heard someone say once that the only people who should have children are grandparents. I think that person had a point."

Max studied her thoughtfully. He noticed that it didn't seem to bother her. She appeared completely relaxed.

"Are you afraid of marriage?" he asked.

"Yes."

"Why?"

"To me, marriage is a complete commitment to another person, body, heart and soul."

"I agree, do you think that's bad?"

"No, but it means caring too much."

"And that's bad?"

"Not bad, but painful."

"Why, I don't think I understand."

"Well, if you care too much for someone, you're too - - - "

"Vulnerable?"

"Yes, that person can hurt you deeply."

"But, can't people hurt each other generally, even when they don't particularly care about each other?"

"I suppose so."

"Do you believe in God, Janene?"

"Yes."

"Do you believe God punishes those who fail him?"

"No. He's a loving, forgiving God."

"Does He expect that same of us if we believe in Him?"

"Yes, I guess so."

"Do you think he is pained and hurt when His people fail Him?"

"Yes."

"Then, how can we follow in His footsteps, being loving and forgiving, if we don't care?"

"I don't know."

"Do you fear being hurt deeply?"

There was no answer. She began to twist her hands nervously for the first time.

"Are you afraid Warren will hurt you?"

"No."

"Because you don't care enough about him?"

"No, that's not true," she said, with considerable agitation. She stood up, nervously pacing across the room.

Warren opened his mouth to speak, but a sharp look from Max halted him. Both men watched her. She started toward the door, then turned and came back to her place on the couch. She asked Warren for a cigarette. He rose to fetch one from the bar. A non-smoker himself, he never carried them. In fact, he had rarely seen Janene smoke, if ever. He lit it for her, and after a couple drags, she seemed to relax again. Sarah Jane chose that moment to enter with a trolley of hot soup, sandwiches and coffee. The conversation switched to general topics, and though she ate heartily, Max and Warren both observed that Janene had little to contribute to the conversation.

After they had finished, and Sarah Jane had removed the remains, Janene rose. She excused herself politely, shook hands with Max Jacobs, and retired to her rooms.

# Chapter 23

The two men sat in silence until a door closed above them. Only then did Warren speak.

"Well, Max?"

"She's still confused, Warren, but I don't think she's particularly depressed. She wanted to appear cynical about marriage and children, and she was rationalizing her fears with the standard clichés. I saw through her with those comments about you. That confused her, because she realized that caring and trusting you made her just as vulnerable to hurt from you, if her theory of caring for someone was to hold water. Based on what I've observed tonight, I think your plan will work. When will you put it into operation?"

"In a few days?" Warren answered vaguely.

Jacobs watched the man intently. Fatigue, worry and pain were visible on Warren's face, but Max saw something else.

"You're in love with her, too, aren't you, Warren?"

"Does it show that much?" Warren agonized.

"Only to someone who knows you well, like I do. Does she know?"

"Yes, and no," Warren replied. "I asked her to marry me around Christmas. She refused, telling me she couldn't marry a man she didn't love. It was then she told me about this other man. Since then, I've made it a point to keep our relationship impersonal."

"Are you going through with it?"

"I have to," was Warren's wretched reply.

"I must get going. Call me if you need anything else."

Warren escorted his friend out, and returned alone. He fixed himself a strong drink. It would take time to put his plan into action, but at the moment, he was beat.

The next morning, Warren was pleasantly surprised when Janene joined him for breakfast. She looked rested and refreshed. She wasn't particularly talkative, but this was not unlike the old Janene. During the course of breakfast, he asked if she'd mind typing some letters for him. She readily agreed, and immediately after breakfast, they set to work.

They broke for lunch at 12:30, and had just finished, when Sarah Jane appeared with a telegram. Since they had taken lunch in the study, neither had heard the doorbell.

Sarah Jane handed the telegram to Warren, and he saw at once it was for Janene. He handed it to her gravely.

Bewildered and frightened, her hands shook as she tore it open, reading the cold, bold words.

Janene Dawson stop Vance shot stop condition critical stop Doctor says stop no will to live stop Asking for you stop please reply stop     Charles

She sat motionless, her eyes glued to the typed message, then she handed it to Warren. He read it quickly, returning it to her. She had not moved nor made any comment.

"What are you going to do?" he asked.

"I'm going, of course," she said without hesitation.

"I thought you didn't want to see him again."

"Oh, Warren," she cried, distress and anguish written on her face. "I can't let him die. Don't you see, it's because of me he doesn't have the will to live. I'd never be able to forgive myself if I just let him die."

"Can you leave him again, should he live?"

"No."

"You'll marry him, then?"

"If he'll have me, yes. Warren, I love him, and God help me, I've just realized how much. Whatever happens, no matter how much it hurts, I want to be with him for as long as it is."

"Do you want me to go with you?"

"No. No. I'll call you if I need you, I promise. You've been so good to me, and I love you dearly. I've been a mess the last few days. I'm sorry. I know why now, and I'm going to be fine. Thanks for everything. I must run and pack." At the doorway, she turned her eyes, bright and shining, her face radiant despite the lines of worry about her mouth and eyes. "Warren, book me a flight to L.A. as soon as possible, then send a telegram. I don't know the address, it's probably on the envelope. If not – Vance Manor, Brea, California. Thank you," she added, dashing back to plant a kiss full upon his lips.

"I'll take care of everything. You go on and pack."

She ran from the room, the door slamming in the wake of her hasty exit.

"Goodbye, Janene, my darling," he said to the closed door. Then, turning to the phone, he dialed Western Union, and requested the following message be sent to Vance Manor, Brea, California.

Mr. Vance Reeves stop Janene coming stop All's well stop You owe me one stop   Fielding

He could only hope Janene would forgive the deception he had perpetrated with the help of Vance Reeves and his aged chauffeur. It wouldn't matter, really, all he needed to know was the only woman he'd ever loved was on her way to happiness. Now the ball was in Reeve's court.

## THE END

Made in the USA
San Bernardino, CA
11 April 2017